Real Time

AMIT CHAUDHURI

Real Time

Stories and a Reminiscence

PICADOR

GREEN

ISBN 0 330 49130 X

"Portrait of an Artist," "Four Days Before the Saturday Night Social,"
"The Man from Khurda District," and "The Great Game" were all
first published in the *London Review of Books*.
"An Infatuation" was published in both the *London Review of Books*
and *The Little Magazine*, where "The Second Marriage" also appeared.
"The Old Masters" appeared in the *London Review of Books* and
Civil Lines 5, which also published "Prelude to an Autobiography."
"Real Time" and "White Lies" first appeared in *Granta*,
and "Words, Silences" in *Man's World*.
"Beyond Translation" was first published in the *New Yorker*, and
"The Party" in the *Times Literary Supplement*.

1 3 5 7 9 8 6 4 2

A CIP catalogue record for this book is available from
the British Library.

Printed and bound in Great Britain by
Mackays of Chatham plc, Chatham, Kent

Contents

Stories

Portrait of an Artist

THE HOUSE WAS in a lane in a middle-middle-class area that curved at a right angle at one end and, at the other, led to the main road. During the Durga Puja, the balconies of the neighbouring houses would be lit with green and blue neon lights, and families would walk towards the end of the lane that curved to the right, and join the crowd that was either coming from or walking towards the goddess. Bank clerks, schoolteachers, small-business men, with their wives and children, the boys in shorts and the girls in frocks, looking like the pictures of children on the covers of exercise books, formed that tireless crowd. On the other side of the lane, after one had crossed the main road, one came to a lake with spacious adjoining walks where couples strolled in the evening and children, accompanied by maidservants, came to play. Binoy and I would walk past the lake in the afternoon, when women washed saris or scoured utensils with

3

ash on its steps, and the heat had just ebbed into a cloudy, dream-like vacancy.

It was in my uncle's house that, during one of my visits, I met my cousin's English tutor, whom they never referred to by name but called "mastermoshai." He was once a manager in an English firm, but had apparently left it after his wife and children had died in a motor accident. After that, he had roamed the streets of Calcutta for a year, seldom returning home, and only lately had he reached, once more, a kind of settled state. He now lived in his house with his servant, Ganesh, and gave English tuition for a small fee to children like my cousins. How he had materialised into my cousins' lives I never really found out, but I gathered that he had been recommended to them by a relative on their mother's side.

When I met mastermoshai I was sixteen years old, and had had a poem published in the *Youth Times,* a magazine now defunct. Prior to the meeting, while I was still in Bombay, my cousins had shown it to him, so that when I arrived, Binoy smiled and said to me, "Mastermoshai was very impressed by your poem." On Saturday morning, I saw a bespectacled man in his early fifties, dressed in a shirt and lungi, enter the small room where Binoy and Robi studied. Approaching the room later, I saw an unlikely lesson in progress, for Binoy and Robi, and even little Mou, were sitting, heads bent, each staring at a book, while the bespectacled man seemed to be reading the exercise books in which they had written their answers. It was a time of particular significance, for Binoy, at fifteen, would be writing his matriculation finals at the end of the year, as would Robi two years later. After the finals, Binoy would have to decide whether he would take Science or Commerce; he would have to be readmitted to his school, or to another school, depending on how well he did, for his upper matriculation exams; and his life would receive an abrupt push towards a certain direction. Even

so, he would not be free of the English language and its literature for at least the next two years, although it would be increasingly marginalised from his life.

So they sat in that room, reading poems by Longfellow or
Tennyson, or short stories by Saki, Binoy the least interested
among them, for his favourite subjects were arithmetic and art,
and his favourite pastime, football. But it said something about
their affection for this man, who sat studying their answers, that
even Binoy had begun to show signs of interest in the English
lesson. Interrupting the tuition at one point, my aunt took me
into the room and introduced me to the tutor. He had a very
Bengali face, with short, slightly wavy hair, a forehead of me-
dium breadth, spectacles that belonged to his face as much as
his eyes did, deep lines around his mouth, and teeth that jutted
out from under his lip, making his face belong to the pre-
orthodontal days. His teeth were tobacco-stained; I was to find
that he, like most Bengali men, smoked constantly. Having now
lived in England for several years, where not many men smoke,
my memory of him taking a long puff on a cigarette is associated
with the anachronistic, old-world atmosphere of Calcutta, with
its small dreams and ambitions. I don't know why I recall his
face in such detail, except that there are some faces, especially
those of men belonging to his generation, that have stayed in my
mind, perhaps because the world that produced them is now
inconceivable. He was not at all handsome, but I see that he
might have been attractive to his wife when he was a young
man. It would have been an attractiveness that is different from
that of the young men of my generation; one has only to see old
Bengali films to realise that men were slighter and smaller in
those days, but with a proportionate elegance and agility.

Robi got up from his chair, and I sat down next to mastermoshai. Robi, sitting on the bed, and Binoy and Mou, looking
up from their books, had formed a small, expectant audience.

Mastermoshai was shy; he was expected to say something about my poem. When two literary men meet in Bengal, they do not ask each other personal questions, but straightaway enter realms of the abstract and articulate. Mastermoshai's first question to me was, in an English accent tempered by the modulations of Bengali speech: "Are you *profoundly* influenced by Eliot?" Though I was taken aback, I countered this with a few names I had recently discovered in the Penguin Modern European Poets series—Mandelstam, Montale, Brodsky. Mastermoshai was impressed. The next time he came to the house, he brought me a novel, a Penguin Modern Classic. It was *Malone Dies* by Samuel Beckett; the copy, he said, belonged to one of his "disciples." The cover had a grim but beautiful picture, a pencil sketch, of a human skull. On the pages inside, difficult words had been occasionally underlined and their meanings noted. A strange world had been described there, one that I could not make sense of. I took the book with me back to Bombay.

It was mastermoshai who first spoke to me of Baudelaire. He knew the names of the French existentialists and the titles of their books—Sartre, Camus, *Being and Nothingness, The Fall*— but his highest praise was reserved for Heidegger's *Being and Time*. The words "being," "subject," "object," frequently entered our conversations, especially when he was discussing my poetry, of which I had begun to produce sizeable quantities. "Every writer needs his Pound," he said to me. "*Il miglior fabbro*— Eliot's better craftsman." He was my first impresario, showing my poem in the *Youth Times* to his friends and "disciples." On another occasion, he compared himself to Leopold Bloom and me to Stephen Dedalus, adding, "Every writer needs a guide, a father figure." On one level, he *was* a father to me, and on another level, a friend. For, behind the big talk about literature, a fondness had grown between us, based on the ardent exchange of ideas that belonged to a foreign language and continent, ideas probably already obsolete over there, but which here, in the comforting presence of relatives and friends, took on a unique intensity, a freshness; a friendship that could have formed only in a country with a colonial past. Even more provincial, and marginal to Europe, than Dublin was in the early twentieth century, was Calcutta at the century's close. Trams, rickshaws, markets, office buildings with wide, creaking stairs, bookshops, little magazines, literary critics, uncles, aunts, created this Dublinesque metropolis of which mastermoshai was a part.

By the time I visited Calcutta again, another one of my poems had appeared in the large, loose-leaf pages of *The Illustrated Weekly of India*. This magazine, easy to roll, generous to the touch, had circulated among members of my mother's family and even reached mastermoshai. He had tucked it under his arm, emerged from my uncle's house, and walked off to show it to his friends—for, in South Calcutta, many literary critics and poets lived within walking distance of one another. "Extraordinarily mature for seventeen years old," Binoy reported him to have said. He was now ready to introduce me to his "contacts," clerks and accountants who led a shadow life as editors, poets, and intellectuals. They were a small, stubborn band of people struggling to keep alive a sense of the urgency of modern poetry and its many movements in the midst of an enervating climate and a society with other preoccupations.

One morning, mastermoshai arrived at my uncle's house. He seemed to be in possession of a secret. He told me to hurry up, for he was taking me to meet the editor of *Living City*. It was a magazine locally published in Calcutta, and I recalled that I had once picked up a copy from a pavement stall in Park Street. I had found it interesting in a strange way, because its contributors were Bengalis I had never heard of, with the kind of common reassuring name you think must belong to learned people—Sukumar Mukherjee, Shibnarain Sen—all writing articles in quaint, textbookish English about Bengali literature and culture. It confirmed my suspicions that the most important work in literature was being done in the regional languages. In Bombay, for instance, I had sensed with some awe that Marathi poets had a highly developed network of meeting places and discussion groups organised around a series of roadside cafés and Irani restaurants. Here, in Calcutta, the contributors to *Living City* seemed more middle class and academic, and yet oddly impressive, inhabitants of a world apart. The editor himself, R. D. Banerjee, had written an article on the Baishnab Padabali, the poets Chandidas and Bidyapati and their influence on Tagore, and the emotions associated with *biraha,* or separation from the loved one or God. In neat boxes by the side of certain pages, there were small poems written in a language that somehow seemed to fit in naturally with the style in which the essays had been written. It was a language that all the contributors to *Living City* had in common, so that one man, almost, might have composed the contents of the entire magazine. There were some pages that had the simplest form of advertisement—a message, or the name of a firm that could not possibly have any interest in literature—personal gestures of goodwill, old friendships, that sustained such a project.

That morning, Binoy and I were relaxing in the house, Binoy in kurta and pyjamas, and I in pyjamas and full-sleeved shirt. Dressed like this, both of us accompanied mastermoshai, in a taxi, to a house in one of the lanes near Southern Avenue, Binoy sitting in the back with mastermoshai, who was singing a Rabindrasangeet, and I, in the front, next to the taxi driver, with one elbow in the open window. In those days, when I came to Calcutta, Binoy took a personal interest in my literary career, and visited, with mastermoshai and me, the houses of several editors, a spectator who silently listened to our discussions and reported them later to my mother and his parents. He had been my closest companion in childhood; we had played and fought with each other. Now, at sixteen and seventeen, he and I were as tall as each other; we had reached our full adult height, though we were still boys. The taxi entered a lane with two- and three-storeyed houses, trees and flowers in their tiny courtyards, their façades in stages of disrepair. It was the time of day when children go to school, and men to their offices, and a domestic calm in which these houses belonged entirely to women and servants was evident as we passed through the lane. To be part of this pre-midday hour was rare for a man. The taxi driver, on master-moshai's command, stopped at a small yellow building. Stone stairs of no particular colour, which we climbed up slowly because of the darkness, mastermoshai our leader, took us past the identical bottle-green doors of the two flats on every floor, till we reached the door which had R. D. BANERJEE in white letters upon a black plastic nameplate. Mastermoshai pressed a buzzer. The three of us stood in the small space that formed the landing at each flight of stairs and the common area outside the flats, a dark square box from which stairs radiated upward and downward. A balding man in spectacles, dressed in a cotton shirt, black trousers, and sandals, opened the door for us. It was Mr. Banerjee himself; politely but tacitly he led us inside. The door, once opened, led to a long corridor that was also a verandah which formed a border to the flat; to its right, there were three rooms with their doors open, and a curtain hanging from each doorway. The verandah ended in a wall, and to its left, there was a rectangular space, and then, the verandah of the opposite flat, with the same three doors. The building thus seemed to enclose an empty rectangle, with the flats on its margins.

Mr. Banerjee took us into the first room through a white curtain with printed flowers. It had a centre table, a small sofa against the wall, two armchairs facing each other, all in a faded green cloth upholstery, wooden shelves with glass panels on the

left, with a few hardcovers upon them. Mr. Banerjee switched
on the fan. There was a window at the other end, with curtains
that were smaller versions of the one at the doorway. Mr. Banerjee sat on the chair at that end, Binoy on the sofa, mastermoshai
next to him, and I on the other armchair. Mr. Banerjee nodded
at Binoy and said to mastermoshai:

"Is he the poet?" Binoy shifted uncomfortably, possibly
wondering, suddenly, what he was doing here. But, dark-
complexioned, almost black, in kurta and pyjamas, large-eyed,
he did look poetic.

"No, no," said mastermoshai. "He is *his* uncle's son. This is
the boy whose poems I showed you." Mr. Banerjee turned to
look at me.

"I see," he said. Unsmilingly, he told me, "I liked your
poems."

Magically, tea and biscuits on a plate arrived from nowhere.
Our presence had set off a small domestic machinery in the flat.
Conversation opened up, and mastermoshai told Mr. Banerjee
more about me, while Binoy sipped his tea and listened.

"I noticed a mood of *biraha* in your poems," Mr. Banerjee
told me. "Have you ever read the Baishnab Padabali?"

"No, I haven't," I said a little hesitantly. "But I am interested.
Could you tell me where I can buy a copy?"

"He has trouble reading Bengali," explained mastermoshai,
"because he grew up in Bombay. As for the Padabali," he said to
me, "you should find it in College Street."

"I will publish your poems next month," said Mr. Banerjee.

Delight made us all silent. We finished our tea, got up to
leave, and mastermoshai thanked him profusely, while Binoy
and I, as before, merged into the background and assumed the
status of bystanders. Mr. Banerjee closed the door, and that was
the last I saw of him.

On my next visit to Calcutta, I found that mastermoshai had

widened his interests; he was thinking of freelancing as a copy-writer and relinquishing his job as a private tutor. He had inserted a small message in the classifieds column of *The Statesman*, advertising his skills and availability, but the message showed such a command of the idiomatic resources of English that it would have been unintelligible to most Bengali readers. One day he came to me and gave me a piece of paper. It was for my father, who worked in a firm that had dealings with Britannia Biscuits. "Ask him to show it to them," he said with great pride and self-assurance. The piece of paper, which seemed blank at first glance, had its entire space filled with three large words written with a ballpoint:

BRITANNIA
IS
BISCUIT

A few days later, he came up with another slogan for one of Britannia's new creations, the orange-flavoured "Delite," and this I liked very much for it spoke to me of his whole personality: "Your taste is our Delite." I handed it to my father, who liked it as well. But once it reached the offices of Britannia Biscuits in Bombay, it was, I think, forgotten.

On my last visit before I left for England, I found that mastermoshai had already left his copywriting days behind and moved on to new things. He had set up a shop with his servant, from which they sold cooking oil to customers. "I've instructed Ganesh," he told my aunt, "to make his hand tremble a little while measuring out the oil." He added, in explanation, "These are hard times." On this occasion, I did not stay in my uncle's house, but in the flat my father had bought many years ago, which now, at last, was furnished. It was the flat to which my parents would move after my father's retirement. My mother told me not to waste my holidays and to make use of my time by taking Bengali lessons from mastermoshai. "After all, he is a learned man," she said. Thus, for the first time, mastermoshai came to our flat. It was a different world inside the flat, but he regarded our affluence and difference without envy; he was not embarrassed or diminished by it. He reminisced to me about a man he had once known, the son of a maharajah, who could no longer step out of his great mansion because he could not understand the world. We sat, in an air-conditioned room, at a study table by a great window that looked out on trees and old, aristocratic houses. The book we began to read together was the slender *Chhelebela,* or *Boyhood,* by Tagore.

"Are you enjoying it?" he asked me at one point.

"I like it very much."

"Of course," he informed me, "you cannot understand, beneath all its lightness, its spiritual rhythm."

I protested then, a little offended. But I know now that he was right, that the music of a piece of writing becomes richer with the passing of time. Mastermoshai's *Chhelebela,* with his life behind him, was not the same as my *Chhelebela,* at the age of seventeen. The Bengali lessons continued, interrupted by discussions in which we spoke of various things, including my most recent poetry, an inexhaustible theme, and the strangely refreshing absence of tragedy in Sanskrit drama. But we did not complete the book. Mastermoshai had a small disagreement with my mother, and then with my uncle, a few childish, irrational outbursts, after which I myself became rather childishly cold with him. It was not a serious breach and would have healed. I met him again, by chance, a few days later in my uncle's house. I had put a record of Hindustani classical music on the gramophone and, listening to it, was waving one arm passionately in the air, keeping time with the music. Unknown to me, mastermoshai came and stood behind me, waving his arms as well. When I saw Binoy smiling, I turned. Mastermoshai stopped immediately and became completely serious. With adult restraint, we acknowledged each other, and he went down the stairs.

Soon after, I left for England. Sometimes I would ask my mother on the phone: "How is Bishnu Prasad Chakrabarty?"—for that was mastermoshai's name. Information about him was scarce, however. It seemed that, after a series of sporadic and silly quarrels, he had left his tuitions and taken up the cooking-oil business in earnest. When I came to Calcutta from England, I longed to make up with him, but no one knew where he was; I heard that he had moved into Ganesh's house beyond the railway lines, where the nomadic poor—domestic servants, factory workers—lived in a different society with a different kind of life. Then, a few years later, my mother told me that he had died, leaving everything to Ganesh. I see now that the period in which I knew mastermoshai was a transitional one, when, after having lost his wife and children, having seen through life, he returned to his youthful enthusiasms—Baudelaire, Eliot—to temporarily regain his sanity. And then, for no good reason, he loosened his ties again.

Since that first meeting, much has changed in my life. Going to England blurred certain things and clarified others. I realised that a strange connection between this small, cold island and faraway Bengal had given rise to the small-town world of Calcutta, and even to mastermoshai; from a distance, I saw it gradually in perspective—a colonial small town, with its trams and taxis, unknown to, and cut off from, the rest of the world, full of a love for the romance of literature that I have not found anywhere else, and that is somehow a vivid part of small-town life. As for Binoy, I hardly see him these days; I live, for most of the year, in another part of the world, while he has stayed on in the house in Calcutta. Not having done exceptionally well at college, he works in his father's business and has also joined, I hear, a political-theatre troupe, and performs, occasionally, in street plays. I saw him once on the stage, dressed in silk and costume jewellery as a medieval king, a turban on his head, his dark face made pale and floury with powder. Calcutta is his universe; like a dewdrop, it holds within it the light and colours of the entire world.

Four Days Before the Saturday Night Social

IT WAS AFTER SCHOOL HOURS. Almost an hour ago, either Krishna or Jimmy had rung the bell, a continual pealing that seemed to release a spring in the backs of the boys and girls, who jumped out of their chairs and proceeded to throw, without ceremony or compassion, their books into their satchels. It was then useless for a teacher to try to be heard, or to beat the table despairingly with the back of a duster, raising dramatic puffs of chalk dust, for the boys hard-heartedly assumed deafness; one or two "good girls" who raised their arms even *now*, a full twenty seconds after the bell, to ask a relevant question, further irritated the teacher, who, her hands powdered with sediments of green and white chalk, wanted to be upstairs in the teachers' common room, pouring tea from her cup into her saucer and very slowly sipping it. Preparing, like Atlas, to lift a tottering load of brown-paper-covered exercise books full of long, ingenious bluffers' answers, she, in a moment of mischief and vindictiveness, said to a "good girl": "Lata, will you please carry these for me upstairs?" So impenitently angelic was the girl that she agreed without a murmur of resentment; with an air of perpetual readiness, even.

Mud-stained boys were now, at half-past four, coming in through the main gate after having played rugger, walking with both a tiptoer's tentativeness and a plodder's crushing stride in their studded boots. Only one girl, but the prettiest of them all, 7D's Charmayne, had stayed back, accidentally, to admire this spectacle. The rugger tryouts had taken the trouble, on-field, during the scrum, to wrestle and hug the earth completely and, by the end of it, to return with an unfaultable cosmetic exterior of dirt, sweat, and plastered hair. Not an inch of clean skin or, on their bodies, uncreased cotton, was to be seen, and on coming through the gate, they were confident of having presented their most redoubtably sluggish, most uncompromisingly slovenly, most acutely male selves to Charmayne's gaze; who, however, refused to look directly at them, perhaps out of shyness.

One of the boys, mounting the two steps to the corridor, regarded his left boot, whose lace had come untied. Elegant, casual, and drooping, the untied lace seemed to him a stylish touch, like an illegible but masterly signature, and he left it as it was and clattered off.

Gautam had stayed back with Khusroo because Khusroo had coaxed him into believing that dancing was something that could be learned. "There are no steps, believe me," he said. "You just have to move, and enjoy yourself." And this matter, of moving, and being able to enjoy it, had taken on some importance because the first Senior School Social of the year had been announced, and the date set for Saturday. "But you *must* come," insisted Khusroo, who had never shown much interest in Gautam's spiritual or social evolution. "You *should* come," he had said with genuine, though inexplicable, eagerness. Gautam had been, at first, resistant. He could not see himself, much as he would have liked to, wantonly positioning himself a few inches away from a girl, and then, with aplomb, shivering and shaking ecstatically before her. Perhaps he would not mind if she did not look at him, but, contradictorily, perhaps he *would* mind. Such introspective furrows were left to be smoothed out by Khusroo, who tried to convince Gautam of the ordinariness and rationality of it—that dance was not a wayward display, but a necessary pleasure. Yet Gautam would not have changed his mind had not Anil, at five feet and half an inch, had the temerity to say, "Of course I'm going," as if it were a right it would be foolish not to exercise. If Anil, at his height, could suffer to relinquish the shield and protection of his white school uniform for the daring intimacy of his social clothes, so could Gautam.

So here they were, standing in the corridor near the gate, in front of one of the Standard 9 classrooms, by the back door to the chemistry laboratory. The temperature had fallen, imperceptibly, gracefully, to 27 degrees, till the school itself seemed raised to a timeless stratosphere that was neither heaven nor earth, a place rained upon by coolness. The sun became tolerant, and suddenly sunlight was reflected in blinks and flashes, now here, now there, off hospital windows across the street that, earlier in the day, no one would have guessed even existed. Just outside the school walls, in the trees whose branches climbed prolifically over roofs and partitions, and ranged freely everywhere like a band of irrepressible trespassers, sparrows had begun to chirp all at once, loudly, excitedly, and perhaps informatively. Now that the school was empty, it seemed that the life around it had begun to imitate the intent, sometimes shy, play of the schoolchildren, with light bouncing and glancing off one hospital window to the next, chasing certain routes and eluding others, and the invisible birds shouting at one another at the top of their voices.

As if he were being rocked from side to side, and backward and forward, in a train compartment, Khusroo's hips and torso shook, as, more frugally, did his legs. "On the shuffeling ma-adness," he sang, "of loco-motive bryeath—da da da all-time loser's hurtlin' to his dyeath . . ." Melody was replaced by a menacing curl of the lips. All the time, Khusroo seemed to lean forward quickly and spectatorially, then immediately retreat backward with a mildly alarmed air; meanwhile, his arms, quite irrelevantly and encouragingly keeping time, appeared to treat these two ostensibly unconnected movements as part of a single motion, accompanying them with magical and peremptory snaps of the fingers. "You try, too," said Khusroo. Gautam, sitting on the floor and looking up, pretended cunningly not to hear. Khus-roo stopped and stamped his foot. "Gautam Bose, what am I do-ing here if you're not going to get up and *do* something?" he said sternly. "Khusroo, I've just realised . . .," mumbled the other. "Realised?" said Khusroo, enraged, as if it had been a particu-larly poorly chosen word. "You haven't *realised* anything! Come on, get up." Gautam obeyed, out of embarrassment; he lifted himself from his brooding inactivity with a giant, ostentatious ef-fort. Then he stood with both his arms by his sides, like a boxer who doesn't know what to do. Khusroo uttered unexpected soothing words: "It's easy, Gautam, just loosen up." But each part of Gautam's body felt like a mechanism that had been jammed and rusted and made useless by shyness and sensitivity, and some miraculous lubricant, like forgetfulness, was now re-quired. He remembered his parents, who, for about two months in the middle of their lives, used to put a 45 r.p.m. on the gramo-phone, and then, in broad daylight, amidst the drawing-room furniture, watched by Gautam looking past the twin peaks of his knees, sitting huddled on the sofa, try out their recently memorised dance steps. His mother, repeatedly adjusting the aanchal on her sari, and saying "Cha-cha-cha" under her breath, as she had no doubt been told to by her instructor, would dance with an expression of utter determination on her face. There were times when, on Gautam's request, she did this when his father was not there, alone, in the drawing room, and the look of determination reappeared. Every Saturday evening, they would go to the first floor of an old mansion behind the Taj Mahal Hotel, where Mr. Sequiera conducted his dancing classes. Mr. Sequiera even advertised on the slides in cinema halls, illuminating this message: BE A SOCIAL SUCCESS: LEARN BALLROOM DANCING! For a while, thus, cha-cha-cha was mentioned in the house, and also that word that could have come straight from a fable: foxtrot. Then, after two months, almost overnight, his parents gave up dance and stopped playing those records and quite calmly took up other habits. Though it is said that children pass through "phases," Gautam found that his parents probably passed through as many phases, if not more, than he did. They were always changing, developing, growing. For instance, when Gautam was eight, his mother would return from the hairdresser with her hair leavened into a full-grown bun, set and lacquered into a marble repose. Now, however, those accessories—hair net, false hair, lacquer spray—were lying in some drawer untouched, and his mother's hair, on evenings out, had taken on another, less extreme, incarnation. His father, too, he remembered, once had two personable sideburns, which, one day, without explanation, had been reduced to a more modest size. There was nothing fixed, constant, or permanent about his parents.

Even as Gautam was summoning within himself the preparedness to set his body moving, without safety, without company, in mid-air as it were, there came a bang from not too far away, and then the sound of a muffled, amplified voice: "Check

. . . one-two-three . . . check." "Come on," said Khusroo, losing
interest in Gautam's lonely fledgling efforts to translate into motion. "Let's see what those chaps are doing. If you don't mind,"
he added, "we'll continue later." "No, no," said Gautam. "No,
let's see what those chaps are doing." They went down the corridor and turned right, and walked a little way to the first door to
the hall. At the other end of the now empty hall, where only this
morning they had stood distractedly with their hymnbooks, the
stage was occupied by the Phantom Congregation, who were
practising, in resounding fits and starts punctuated by gaps of silence and slouching, the songs that would set this hall and the
bones and vertebrae of various eager neophytes vibrating next
Saturday. Rahul Jagtiani, the lead singer, a tall, unextraordinary
boy with spectacles and a moustache, was holding the mike with
one hand casually, as if it were a perfectly mundane, everyday
object, and talking to Keki Antia, the bassist, who, as he struck
the strings on his guitar with his plectrum, produced fat, pon-
derous globules of sound. The other two were bent upon their
instruments in introspective postures of study and absorption:
the thin, spirit-like, demoniacally stubble-cheeked Freddy Billimoria, who leaned with a mixture of swooning pleasure and fatigue over his drums, now thudded, with a pedal at his foot, the
great bass drum standing upright, and now, superfluously, hit the
floating cymbal with a polished attenuated stick that seemed a
fitting extension of his own skinniness, creating a marvellous
sound that rippled outward, a reverberating whisper. And Rajat
Kapoor, also splenetic and unpredictable, hit his guitar strings
at times to release that loud electric bang that Khusroo and
Gautam had heard from a distance, which they now understood
to be a particular chord. Then he would rapidly turn one of the
four knobs on the guitar's incandescent flame-red box and prick
his ears for a prophetic hum on the speaker. To Khusroo's and
Gautam's awe, Rahul Jagtiani suddenly turned and exclaimed,

"Hey—one-two-three," and all those individual technological noises were gathered into a single united wave, and they began to sing "Smoke on the water, fire in the sky." The combined voices of Antia, Jagtiani, and Billimoria could hardly be heard over Rajat Kapoor's guitar, which had been, midway through the song, launched into the wayward kinks and corkscrew effect of the wa-wa mode. Khusroo and Gautam felt jolted by the scruff of their necks and shoulders, a cavity forming in their solar plexus, and they looked on speechless with wonder.

The stage was not always such a profane site. In fact, in the morning, at nine o'clock, the Principal stood upon it and took the lead in folding his hands together and, uncharacteristically, closing his eyes to say, rather haltingly, the Lord's Prayer. Gautam knew only some of the words—"vouchsafe," "Almighty God," "daily bread" (when he involuntarily and quite logically pictured a white Britannia slice), and the incomprehensible last lines, "Thy kingdom come, Thy will be done, on earth as it is in heaven, forever and ever, Amen." The other words in the prayer, which far outnumbered these intervals of continuity, he substituted with approximate reverent vowel and consonant sounds. On some mornings, the head boy, or even a house captain or prefect, read out the prayer with a zeal and a correctness of elocution which the Protestant Principal from Kerala himself lacked. These prefects possessed an enviable purposefulness of bearing that told one there were no stains on their conscience, and that an awareness of duties, theirs and others', was never far from their minds; and they carried out, whenever they could, the Principal's and even the Lord's will in school. To the ordinary boys and girls in class, however, God was a figure whose qualities were daily advertised and who was deferred to each morning, but who, in their lives, they had discovered through an inuring process of trial and error, was an absent friend, a perpetually missing advisor, and an unreliable and niggardly petitionee.

On Thursday mornings, Father Kurien, in a long white habit, looked down apocalyptically upon the heads of the boys and girls and, doubling the size of his own eyes, fulminated about a God who had eyes everywhere, or lowered his voice to make gentle, ironical jabs at Darwin's theory of evolution. He had a flowing Malayali accent, where one consonant, without quite ending, liquidly siphoned off into another—"m," for instance, became "yem."

At least once a week, nationalistic ideals were indulged by reading out "Where the Mind Is Without Fear." The entire hall, then, in a grave, communal, drowsy chorus, said the words together; from afar, it would have sounded like nothing human, like a host of spirits praying, a murmur that swelled and died and swelled again:

> Where the mind is without fear and the head is held high;
> Where knowledge is free;
> Where the world has not been broken up into fragments by
>   narrow domestic walls;
> Where words come out from the depth of truth;
> Where tireless striving stretches its arms towards perfection;
> Where the clear stream of reason has not lost its way into
>   the dreary desert sand of dead habit;
> Where the mind is led forward by Thee into ever widening
>   thought and action—
> Into that heaven of freedom, my Father, let my country
>   awake.

Before the crescendo of the last line, when Gautam woke with a thrill of guilt, and, simultaneously, a surprisingly genuine, perhaps ungrateful, stab of hatred towards Tagore, before that line Gautam let his mind wander, here and there, from the Marine Drive, to Jerry Lee Lewis, to two girls in 7A, Jasmine and Padmini, to his mother's bye-bye in the morning, to Mr. Patke, the P.E. teacher. On those unusual but inevitable days when Gautam's mind found that it had recklessly and unwisely expended all its thoughts and had nothing more to think about, it had to return, prodigally, bankruptly, to the poem, where it clung with lowly fingers to whatever was concrete and material in the midst of all that fatherly high thinking and abstraction; thus, odd pictures flashed before its eye, of people walking upright with their heads thrust backward; of a row of ten-foot walls coming up and then being demolished by someone (perhaps Tagore) with a sledgehammer; of bedouins, tents, and mysterious desert landscapes.

When they were out in the corridor again, Gautam said to Khusroo, "You think they take drugs?" Khusroo snorted: "Those chaps? I doubt it, my dear fellow. They're not even sixteen." The music followed them out into the corridor and took on an independent, if less coherent, life there. "Jim Morrison was a tripper," he said warmly. "But no one knows what happened to him." They walked past the small quad, where NCC cadets marched to "daine baye daine baye," on Fridays. On the wall at that end, which separated the school from the Gyan Sadhana College of Science and Commerce, founded by B. R. Ambedkar for the "scheduled castes," a black-and-white cat, poised in profile, had actually paused to turn its face towards the noise in the corridor before it jumped down lightly into the abyss on the other side. Two crows hopping on the even black ground of the quad had been taken aback by the noise that seemed unrelated to the usual belligerence of hockey sticks and rubber balls in the area; unable to locate its source, they darted around together, shooting quick, investigative glances in the wrong direction, not yet ready to fly off. Urchin boys in khaki shorts and shirts with one or two buttons left were standing by the main gate of the school, grinning, but not daring to come in. The music had reached here, softer but still clear, joyous, contrasting with the tiny everyday sounds of the hospital, the college, and the rest of the lane. The two began to go up the stairs, stomping recklessly and making as much noise as they pleased, passing a room next to the vice principal's office where question papers for a terminal exam were being unhurriedly cyclostyled. As they went past, they saw one of the hamaals, Fernandes, no longer in his khaki uniform but wearing grey trousers and a terylene shirt, sitting on a stool, his hand cupped round a beedi, smoke issuing from his nostrils. There were no teachers around—only the vice principal, Mr. Pascal, lived upstairs in a flat no one had ever seen, with his wife and children, who too were unknown figures. Yet it was said that Mr. Pascal sometimes descended the stairs at six o'clock with a rifle in his hand, strode to the centre of the empty quad where, during the day, they played basketball, and shot at the pigeons decreed to be a nuisance in school.

Fifteen years later—though they did not know it—they would be in different parts of the world, having become quite different people; Khusroo, so popular with girls and so enviably familiar with them, would discover in Texas that he was "gay," a word that had still not entered their vocabulary, except briefly in the line "A Poet could not but be gay"; Gautam would study chartered accountancy in London and never return home; Anil would become a playwright in English; Freddy Billimoria's moustache would darken; he would lose his thinness and become regional (Asia) manager of an American corporation; Charmayne would get married and have two children and open an aerobics class; no one would know where Rahul Jagtiani was; the few who remembered him would still be able to recall with some difficulty the bird-like cry of his guitar.

"Apparently he's gunrunning in the Congo," said Khusroo of Jim Morrison, who got all his information from his elder brother Darius, a formidably knowledgeable individual whom Gautam had glimpsed only once or twice, a person who possessed a quirky, almost spiritual beauty that was incarnated in the silvery braces he shifted uncomfortably, every few minutes, in his mouth, and the two or three small, inflamed red pimples that were scattered on his cheeks. "With Rimbaud." "Rambo?" said Gautam, never before having heard a name that sounded like that. "Not Rambo, Rimbaud," said Khusroo through his nose. Both Khusroo and his best friend, Anil, were Gautam's guides through the echoing, fantastic-hued chambers of rock music; they talked, Gautam listened; but behind all the words was the distant, intransigent, instructive, bespectacled figure of Darius. It was Darius who had first brought to their small worlds the intractable poetic name of Frank Zappa; it was Darius who had informed them of the subtle but fluid difference between "bop" and "jazz"; it was Darius who set off colourful fusions of images in their heads by declaring that the walrus in "I Am the Walrus" was John Lennon, and that "Sexy Sadie" was the Maharishi: Darius spoke the words; Khusroo and Anil merely repeated. Since then Gautam had entered a pink-green world of innuendoes and monsters, culminating in his purchase of *Sgt. Pepper's Lonely Hearts Club Band* from Rhythm House, with rows of famous heads, dead ones and living ones, arranged on the cover like a great floral bouquet, a gift, and at the back, at the bottom, near "Printed in Dum Dum, Calcutta," the words he had almost missed: "A splendid time is guaranteed for all." They went now into their classroom and slung their satchels on their backs. They had a lot to talk about as they went down the stairs.

It seemed that there was nothing Gautam could do about going to the dance on Saturday. Already he was thinking of the trousers he would wear. Last year his mother had had two pairs of polyester trousers made for him by Woodrow and Bayne, his father's tailors, but they were too formal. For a long time he had searched for trousers that would fit him tightly around the thighs; he had heard that hippies who had come to India in search of enlightenment sometimes sold their Levi Strausses and Wranglers outside the Stiffles Hotel; they were the real thing, with faded furry patches shining against the inky blue like velvet. But his mother, always one to criticise new ideas and bent on doing everything according to her own, rather limited, understanding, had said the jeans might not be safe because the hippies often had diseases. His mother, ever since he could remember, saw germs, uncleanliness, and infection everywhere, in the most innocent of things, in the rims of glasses, in wet plates, in fingers, especially dark brown ones, and had taken it upon herself to battle her way through a country whose citizens possessed immune systems that were always on their toes. And then someone had told him that a shop in Kemp's Corner was making blue jeans, the first in India. He had gone there one hopeful morning with his mother, and, after trying out a pair, had said, "Will it fade?" Yes, he had been assured, the colour would run. They were altered again by another tailor to hug his thighs, and now he wore no other trousers at all, and one could see him in them when he went out with his parents for drives, or with Anil for walks down Breach Candy, or to pick his father up from office. It was not that his mother did not throw tantrums about the other two trousers, or try to part Gautam from these, she and Jamuna smuggling them away and both maintaining they were being dry-cleaned at the laundry, until Gautam became suspicious. But now, for the first time, he would wear them to school. Everyone would come wearing clothes he had never seen them in before, in T-shirts, real Levi Strauss jeans, and Charmayne in a backless halter.

The Man from
Khurda District

BISHU HAD LIVED in Calcutta for eight years but still couldn't speak proper Bengali. "I does my work," or "I am tell him not to do that," he would say. Even so, he courted his wife in precisely this language and then married her. With his child he spoke in either Oriya or his version of Bengali, and the child, now a year and a half old, did not seem to mind.

He was twenty-seven years old. His elder brother, Mejda—"Middle Elder Brother"—a cook's helper in the Bengal Club, had arranged this job for him as a sweeper and cleaner in a house in Ballygunge. Mr. Banerjee, owner of the large two-storeyed house, had divided it equally into four flats, in one of which he lived with his wife, giving the other three out for rent. Thus, this house, a long white rectangular structure with a huge lawn recumbent before it, had still not been sold or torn down, as so many mansions of the once privileged classes in this area had, giving way to multi-storeyed buildings, ITC-owned flats, Marwari-built houses that were a grotesque mishmash of ancient European and futuristic architectural styles. Instead, it had recently been repainted. The house just next to it, a lovely yellow mansion with a drooping banyan tree in the courtyard, was supposed to have belonged to a descendant of the Tagore family and had lately been turned into a UNESCO office—but, thankfully, not destroyed. Bishu and his family lived in a room on the first floor of the servants' outhouse near the white mansion.

One day Mr. Banerjee called for Bishu and said to him:

"Bishu, I'm looking for a man to look after the compound and to help the mali—a good man. Can you look out for one?"

Bishu listened carefully, shyly, and said:

"I tries, dadababu. I sees if I finds someone."

Then he went back to his work and, thinking about it, realised that what dadababu wanted was a replacement for Ratan, the errand boy who had left suddenly three months ago.

That Sunday, he left Uma, his wife, and his child at home in the outhouse and went to Esplanade to meet his elder brother.

"Why can't Mejda come here?" asked Uma irritatedly. She was holding the child in her arms. It was quite large for its age, and was quiet and dark-skinned and pretty, and had immense eyes that were now looking out at something through the window over Uma's shoulder.

"In club Mejda has work every day—how will he come?" Bishu said. He had to be a little extra assertive, or else he knew that Uma, who was older than he was, wouldn't let him go.

"Then you come back by four, or I'll be gone to Meeradi's house," she challenged. She seemed certain of her decision.

"You go," he said, and left.

The tram to Esplanade was fairly empty, and as it rattled

along slowly, Bishu sat on a seat on the left and looked out of the window. People kept coming in and getting out. When the tram came to Esplanade, he got off and saw his Mejda standing in front of a shop with its shutters down.

"Ei, Mejda!" he called, and went up to him.

"Ei, Bishu!" said Mejda, and put an arm around him. "Tell me—what work brings you here?"

Bishu loved talking to Mejda because it was Mejda who had taken the first step out of the village in Orissa—they belonged to the sweeper caste—and had come to Calcutta. He now had a "permanent" job in the Bengal Club, and was a kind of guardian to Bishu. They walked together away from the Esplanade area and K. C. Das, going down the road that led to the All India Radio building and the Governor's house.

"What about the Money Order?" asked Mejda. "Borda wrote to me and said he had got no M.O. from you last month."

"That's right," said Bishu. "Priti was sick, and there was a lot of expenditure. I had to take her to a doctor. But this month I've sent a hundred." The usual amount he sent his eldest brother and mother was seventy-five rupees.

"Crops weren't good this year," said Mejda, as if explaining why Borda had sent him the letter.

"Everywhere there are problems," said Bishu. "In the village there are problems, in the city there are problems."

As they walked on side by side, Mejda a little taller, his pace more leisurely, Bishu quick-stepped, they discussed their youngest brother, Amal, a reckless boy who was in serious trouble in the village. Some people were saying that he or another boy had made a girl pregnant, though he was apparently less directly involved than the friend; nevertheless, he had fled to another village.

"That boy is always causing trouble," said Mejda, somewhat tolerantly.

"Best thing to get him out of Khurda and bring him to Calcutta," said Bishu.

They concurred. Then Mejda asked, "Bishu, are you hungry?" "Why, haven't you eaten, Mejda?" "Work finished at three—I had no time to eat." "Yes, I'm hungry," said Bishu, as if merely deciding he was would make him so.

They had come to Dacre's Lane, and they pushed past people coming from the opposite direction, and past fruit sellers sitting on the side. In kodai after kodai, aubergines in batter were being fried, men were fanning the smoke, in some stalls mutton and chicken rolls were being made on a tavaa. Mejda wanted to eat at the Chinese stall, where they served chili chicken and noodles—although, in spite of the fact that he worked in the Bengal Club, he had only a vague idea this food was Chinese. A man in a dhoti and vest served them the food, and they sat and ate on the benches on one side.

Afterwards, full, and with beedis in their hands, they re-emerged from Dacre's Lane and walked towards Red Road. They sat down beneath the statue of the Unknown Soldier, a British Tommy. People passed by, families, children making strange noises that now denoted pleasure, now curiosity, now anger. At one point, Bishu said: "Mejda—babu was saying, Is there a man to do some work in the garden and help the mali and, you know, do odd jobs?" Mejda looked thoughtful and then said: "I'll see, Bishu. There is a man from our district, Jagan, he seems trustworthy. I used to know him in the village, and he's related to my wife's maternal uncle. I know he's here in Calcutta and out of a job. I'll see if I can send him to you." A balloon seller went past, and Bishu called out "Ei" to him, and the balloon seller came back to him rubbing a balloon, and said, "Yes, dada?" "I'll buy one for Priti," said Bishu to Mejda, a little ashamed. "Priti—my little Priti?" Mejda sounded offended. "I will buy it," he said. He chose one that was a composite of two balloons, shaped like a bird, with a beak and paper eyes stuck to its head. "Yes—how much is this?" he asked. The balloon seller rubbed the bird and said, "Eight annas." "Eight annas—son of a bitch—for that thing?" said Mejda, taking out a coin from his pocket. He spat on the ground. The balloon seller smiled with betel-stained teeth as he untied the balloon. Bishu took it home.

"DADABABU," whispered Bishu.

Mr. Banerjee was sitting on a sofa with a magazine in his hand. He was smoking a pipe. When Bishu repeated the call, he looked up.

"Dadababu," said Bishu, and grinned shyly, as if he had won a prize, "I brings a man—you tells me—to help mali."

Mr. Banerjee looked absently at him for a few seconds. He had been reading of a takeover bid in Bombay and of obstruction to future investment in Calcutta. His father had been a well-known businessman in the days of successful Bengali business, but he himself had done a modest though not unimportant job in a company.

"Oh, you've brought a man," he said at last.

"Yes, dadababu," said Bishu, happy that Mr. Banerjee's attention had focused upon him. He glanced behind him.

A man who had so far been in the background stepped forward—a thin man with a lined face, his hair combed backward; he was not more than forty years old. He bowed briefly to Mr. Banerjee. "Namashkar, shaheb," he said. Mr. Banerjee, pipe in one hand, said to Bishu:

"You know this man?"

"Oh yes!" said Bishu, smiling broadly again. "He is from Khurda district—our district, dadababu!"

"What is your name?" asked Mr. Banerjee.

"Jagan, dadababu," said the man, bending a little.

He was wearing a yellow cotton shirt and a dhoti.

"You have some experience?" said Mr. Banerjee. He glanced at his wristwatch, because he had to go out.

"I am working for two years at house in Ballygunge Circular Road as watchman," said the man.

"Then why did you leave?" asked Mr. Banerjee. Glancing at him, one could see he had been out of work for some time.

"Dadababu, children went to America and babu sold house to company," said the man.

"What is his name?" said Mr. Banerjee.

"Bhattacharya," said Jagan.

"Bhattacharya . . . Where is he now?"

"He moved to flat in Landsdowne Road," said the man.

Mr. Banerjee sighed and said:

"I will put you to work as mali's helper on three hundred rupees. If you work, you will get a raise in salary. When can you start?"

"I will start right now," said the man. "Only, babu, three hundred rupees is too little, I have two daughters in the village . . ."

Mr. Banerjee waved him away.

"Start now, and we will see."

When they came out of the house, Bishu walked across the lawn and Jagan followed him. The lawn was green and bright. They came to the outhouse, and Bishu took him inside to a room on the right that was adjacent to the stairway to the first storey. It was a small bare room with sunlight coming through the barred window, and it had a narrow bed. "You'll stay here," he said. Jagan put the silver-coloured trunk he was carrying on the ground.

"Where can I have a bath?" he asked Bishu.

"There is a bathroom and toilet near the garage," said Bishu. "I'll show you. Do you want to bathe now?"

The man nodded and smiled.

"I've travelled a long way and I want to get the dust off my body."

"Then come with me," said Bishu.

He shoved the trunk carefully beneath the bed, and walked back with Bishu across the lawn towards the back of the white house. Sunlight was in the air.

"Did Mejda send any message?" asked Bishu.

"He was only asking me tell you that he is well," replied the man.

"Where were you staying before this?"

"Near Shyambazaar. Very far," said Jagan, smiling.

When they came to the bathroom near the garage, Jagan shrugged off his shirt and went in.

"NEW MAN IS COME TODAY," said Bishu to his wife.

He was sitting on his haunches on the floor, with his back to the bed. Uma was stirring something on the stove, and its smell had filled the room.

"Where is he staying?" she asked.

"He is downstairs," he said. He got up from the floor. "Let me see if he is there. He might want eating some daal." And swiftly he had gone down the stairs, and he came back slowly after a couple of minutes. "He's not there."

The child was sleeping on the bed with her thumb in her mouth. Bishu squatted on the floor again and said:

"I thinks about bringing my brother Amal from the village. I was speaking to Mejda about it." He looked at her defensively, expecting an outburst. But she went on stirring the pan; in the cup of one palm she collected some onion peelings and threw them out of a window on the right.

"Where will he stay?"

She had never seen any of Bishu's family except Mejda. She

and Bishu had married two years ago, in secret, after a brief courtship in this lane. She had been working in the big multi-storeyed building opposite, on the seventh floor. She had left the job one day and got married without telling didimoni, although didimoni had always been kind to her. But now she was back on good terms with her and visited her from time to time. She had been married once before, but her husband had already had a wife, and so she left the village and came to Calcutta. At the time of her marriage to Bishu, she was already pregnant, and she had had Priti a few months later.

"I asks dadababu," said Bishu guiltily. "Maybe he gives Amal some work."

"Wake the child," said Uma. "She has to eat."

THE NEXT NIGHT, it began to rain again. It was late July, the middle of the monsoons, but it had been so hot over the last four or five days that everyone had almost forgotten the rains; it felt like April. But now, at night, it began to rain again with the intensity it had had before, as if to remind people that the monsoons had not gone away. There were flashes of lightning that illuminated the small room on the first storey, Uma's figure on the bed, sleeping in her sari, with the child, a smaller and darker shadow by her side, seeming even more deeply asleep, unilluminated by the lightning. When there were those vast unexpected rumbles of thunder, the room seemed to shake, and the sky seemed to be falling on it.

"Close that window," said Uma, still no more than an outline.

"Always raining . . . always raining," muttered Bishu.

He got up from the mattress on the floor and went to the window; a cool wind blew onto his face. He pulled the window; already the ledge was wet, and he saw that the rain had begun to blur the lamppost opposite. When he closed the window, the room became darker, but all night it continued to thunder and the sound of rain could be heard. Although Bishu feared the rains and the damage they could do, he was also glad, because it had become cooler and he slept more comfortably.

The next morning the sun was out, but there were puddles of water on parts of the lawn. The sour-faced old mali, in a dhoti and a shirt, was bent over the plants and muttering something. Leaves and branches had fallen on the side of the driveway and had to be thrown away; the birds in the trees had returned to their normal life and business and could be heard all day. But, once more, that night it rained, and it continued to rain, on and off, for the next ten days. It brought chaos to the lane, Southern Gardens, and morning would begin with drivers shouting at each other and car horns being blown because water had collected at the entrance to the lane and made getting out difficult. "Now it's really begun," thought Bishu. The days were monochromatic and dull, with light like a suggestion. Then, on the tenth day, when the rain had reduced to a drizzle and there was sun and rain at the same time, the mali shouted to Bishu as he was passing by the lawn, "Ei Bishu, where's that man of yours?" Bishu stopped. "Which man, dadu?" he asked. " 'Which man, dadu?'— why, that Oriya you brought here—I haven't seen him for the last three days! Has he come here to work or sleep?" "I'll see, dadu," mumbled Bishu, and went off quickly, ashamed. After all, he was a man from his district; but, come to think of it, Bishu hadn't seen much of Jagan during the last seven days, either, though that could be because he had been busy with other things during the rains; anyway, he worked inside the house and returned to his room only in the evening. But he decided he would look into Jagan's room later.

In the evening, before going upstairs, he stood outside Jagan's door and called: "Jaganda, are you there?" A voice came from inside: "I'm here." Bishu went in, saying, "It's just that mali was asking me about you—he hasn't seen you for a few days." Jagan was lying on the bed; he said, "I began to feel ill two days ago, and I haven't been well—it's these rains." His voice was hoarse, and Bishu went up to him and felt his forehead. "You have fever," he said. "Yes, it came a few days ago," said Jagan, "but it's getting better." "Okay, then you rest tomorrow," said Bishu, turning around to leave. Then he saw a mat rolled up against the wall, and Jagan said, "My aunt's son is staying with me for a few days. He needs a place to stay, and I told him to stay with me for a few days. I don't know the ways of this place—is it all right?" Bishu thought for a few seconds; he knew it wasn't done, but he decided not to give it too much importance. "It's all right, Jaganda," he said. "You don't worry."

One night the following week, when Bishu had returned to the outhouse after some work in the mansion, he noticed three bicycles on the landing, leaning on the wall by the staircase. They seemed quite new; the bicycle spokes glinted sharply in the light of the bulb. Bishu wondered what they were doing there—had the watchman put them there? No, it must be Jagan. He listened outside Jagan's door, but there seemed to be no one inside the room.

He went up to his room, and a little later Uma brought him his dinner of rice and daal and vegetables. He ate without talking much, thinking of whether he should tell Mr. Banerjee about the bicycles. "Something seems to be on your mind," said Uma. "No, it is nothing," he said, rising to wash his hands. "Nothing." He decided to dismiss the thought from his head.

THEN A HOT SPELL BEGAN AGAIN, punctuated by infrequent showers. It was during hot days like these that Bishu had first met Uma two and a half years ago. Uma used to emerge from the gates of the building opposite, Southern Gardens Flats, and walk down the lane towards the main road, perhaps going to the market; on her way she would stop at the gate of the strange new, huge Marwari house, which looked like something between a castle and an aeroplane, and talk to the watchman, whom she seemed to know. Bishu, who was never really friendly with the servants in the house he worked in, loitered about a lot, and he had seen her a few times. She was not particularly pretty; she was thin (though not as thin as she was now), with protruding teeth; but, in her sari, she looked slim and small and had a certain grace.

Often she would come down the path that went past the outhouse with a pitcher against her waist. One day Bishu said to her:

"What's the matter, don't you getting water in your building?"

"Of course we do—why shouldn't we?" said Uma. "It's just that didimoni prefers tubewell water."

Bishu noticed that there was vermilion in the parting of her hair: he realised she had a husband somewhere, in either her past or present; he was not unduly bothered. Thus their courtship began, fifteen or twenty minutes of conversation each day on the dusty path between the outhouse and the mansion that led to the tubewell, looked upon and ignored by the many windows and verandahs, the numerous eyes, of the multi-storeyed building. Sometimes she had a ponytail, sometimes a plait. Their differences—he an Oriya of the sweeper caste, she a once married Bengali—which should have kept them apart, only brought them together. In a couple of months, the conversations had led to the first physical intimacy in the room in the outhouse, hurried embraces; though everything was so quickly and secretively done that no one had an inkling, least of all didimoni. It was only after Uma had begun to retch and throw up and realised she was pregnant that she ran away from her job to marry Bishu.

AFTER A SHORT BURST of rain late in the morning, the sun came out and it became hot again. Priti, who either played with other children on the dusty path where her parents had once met, or wandered about at home, was now crawling about busily in the room, seeming to have found a playmate in the sun, which, though burning in the sky after the shower, appeared to be crawling about in the room as well. Her mother picked her up and put her on the bed, where she sat without protesting. A few minutes later, two shaliks came to the window.

"Paati!" said Priti, looking at them, for all birds were pakhi, or "bird," to her. The birds took off immediately, and Priti seemed a little surprised that they were now here and now not. When her mother picked her up and took her to the window, she looked out at the lane contentedly, with its buildings and huge banyan and gulmohur trees casting shadows everywhere.

In the afternoon, Uma took the child in her arms and went to visit didimoni on the seventh floor of Southern Gardens Flats. She did this from time to time, because she was always welcome in didimoni's flat and she liked to keep in touch with her.

"Oh—it's Uma," said Mrs. Sengupta, whom Uma called "didimoni." "Come into the room! How are you?"

"I'm well, didimoni," said Uma shyly, stepping inside the bedroom. She sat on the floor beside the bed, Priti in her arms.

"The child has become very sweet—pretty . . . ," said didimoni.

Uma smiled with pleasure; that was another reason she liked coming here—the child was always fussed over. Priti looked back at didimoni and around her in silence, as if puzzled by the flat.

"And is everything going well?" asked Mrs. Sengupta.

"What should I say, didimoni," said Uma with a small smile, "sometimes I want to leave him and come back here with Priti to work—he bothers me at times!"

Didimoni laughed—but did not know what to say. For although she could have possibly given Uma a job, it would have been too much of a problem having a child in the house; she had tried it with another servant, and it hadn't worked. Nor did she really take Uma's complaint seriously. And yet her heart went out to her. She had become thinner than before, and darker, and her teeth seemed to protrude from her mouth more prominently.

"Never mind," she said, thinking back to her own marriage. "There are always misunderstandings at first, and then they get smoothed out." Uma nodded and smiled a little, while Priti, in her arms, looked this way and that. Uma remembered how, in the first days she had met Bishu, she used to think he was a driver, because he sometimes had the car keys in his hand; only later had she discovered he was a cleaner.

After half an hour, she got up and said goodbye to didimoni, promising to come again, and walked to the front door and then the lift, glimpsed by the cook and the other servant who had once been her companions in this flat. On her way out, the child in her arms looked in a leisurely way at the furniture in the house—it was difficult to tell if she was registering anything—as if content to be adrift in this frail maternal carriage, an avid, if powerless, observer of life.

IN THE MIDDLE OF SEPTEMBER, towards the end of the rains, Mr. Banerjee threw a couple of dinners in his flat. An unusual brightness emanated from that side of the mansion; parties were seldom thrown these days. Behind the white façade of the mansion, the lives of the occupants were in a sort of abeyance; none of the tenants paid rent to Mr. Banerjee—and Mr. Banerjee did not seem terribly concerned. Only against one tenant was a court case under way.

One morning, when Bishu was walking past the lawn towards the lane to buy a few things from the tea stall, the Hindustani watchman at the gate called out to him. "E Biswajeet!" They had never really liked each other, and the watchman always addressed him by his full, not his shortened, name. He was a bulky man in khaki, certainly larger than Bishu, who was only five feet four inches, and he had moustaches. "Have you heard?" "Heard what, darwan?" asked Bishu. "I haven't heard anything." "Arrey, everyone has heard and you haven't heard," said the watchman. "You're a strange fellow! Your friend was taken away this morning by the police." "My friend?" said Bishu—he felt suddenly ill; he could not hear the raucous cries of the crows overhead. "Which friend?" "Arrey—which friend—that friend of yours, Jagan, the one you brought to work," said the watchman, leaning back on his stool. The watchman, his uniform, the lane, Southern Gardens, the sunlit lawn, all seemed to belong to a world of which Bishu was not really part. "Why?" he asked softly. "What does he do?" "The fellow is a thief, a known thief—he and his aunt's son and some others were stealing bicycles and other things and selling them in these parts. They opened his trunk and found a gun in it—I saw it myself! Where did you bring him from, e Biswajeet?"

The first thing Bishu did was go back to Jagan's room and open the door; the room was completely bare, except for sunlight and shadows coming through the window. Then he went upstairs, and Uma came out of the door and said, "Where were you? Mali was looking for you." "Why he looking for me?" asked Bishu, stepping inside. Daal was boiling on the stove, and Priti was sitting on the floor and slapping it with her small hands. "How should I know? Is he an easy man to talk to? He just mumbled something and went off—I think dadababu wants to see you."

Later, when Bishu met Mr. Banerjee in the sitting room inside his flat, he found the latter had already taken a decision.

"Bishu," he said, "I asked you to bring me a *good* man. Did you know Jagan was stealing bicycles?"

Bishu wondered if he would lie, but he swallowed, and nothing would come out except what had really happened.

"One night, dadababu," he said, "I sees bicycles. But I don't asks Jagan, because after rains he has fever, and I don't disturb him."

"Why didn't you tell me, Bishu?" asked Mr. Banerjee.

"Dadababu, I don't see the bicycles again. I—I forgets them," said Bishu. "I don't realise . . ."

"This morning," said Mr. Banerjee, "the police asked me if any of the servants were involved with that man. I could have told them your name, but I didn't. But, taking into consideration what has happened, I don't think I can keep you in this house any longer."

Bishu was standing barefoot, his hands behind his back, staring at the floor. Then he said:

"Dadababu, I do not knows this man. When you tells me, 'Get me good man,' I tells Mejda, and he says: 'I sends man from Khurda district, I knows him, he is from our village, he is good man.' I not knows the man, dadababu."

"Be that as it may, you should have been more careful," said Mr. Banerjee. "I can keep you no longer."

Bishu was silent. Then, looking at the floor, he said again:

"Dadababu, I works for seven years in this house, this is my first mistake. Please forgive me . . . I never gives you trouble before. Last year, you goes out of Calcutta for one month and didi alone in the house. If I thief, I could steal then from the house, but I does not steals anything. Please forgive me this time."

"I can't change my mind, Bishu," said Mr. Banerjee. "You will have your full month's salary and your notice."

When Bishu got back to his room, he sat on the floor and repeated every detail to Uma; Uma listened silently, while Priti still sat nearby, absorbed, playing. He slapped his forehead with his hand, and said, "That serpent was always in our house, and I does not know it? Hai, what happened!" He could not even properly remember Jagan anymore, just the yellow check shirt and the dhoti he had worn on the day of arrival, and his ordinary, lined face, a face like so many others, of people struggling and arriving in this city and looking for work. "The man is a serpent! Quietly stealing bicycles, and I does not know! There was gun inside his trunk!" he said, as if he himself had seen it, which he now thought he had, so clear and vivid and treacherous it seemed to him. "Now, when I thinks of it, I never sees him in his room when I comes back at night—he must be doing all his dirty business at night!" Then he said, angry and hurt: "Dada-babu blames me! I does nothing, but, for no reason, he tells me to go! No, I does not want this job!" The injustice of it shocked him. Uma could hear the cries of shaliks and mynahs and crows increasing with the afternoon. She felt sorry for Bishu, who was, after all, younger than she, and on whom the burden of his small family had fallen unexpectedly.

Evening was full of activity. Bishu went to his friends in the building at the end of the lane, South Apartments, which was even bigger and more impressive than Southern Gardens Flats—it had come up two years ago. He told his friends to see if there were any jobs available. It turned out that a Mr. Chatterjee in one of the flats needed a helper in the house, and one of Bishu's friends took him to see the gentleman. Mr. Chatterjee saw Bishu and did not dislike what he saw; it appeared there might be a chance for a job. Meanwhile, Uma, carrying Priti in her arms, went to didimoni to tell her of what had happened. Didimoni was aghast. "But what will you do now?" she asked. "The worst that can happen is we will go to Manecktala where we used to pay rent for a room. That room is still there," said Uma. Mr. Sengupta, didimoni's husband, said: "Bishu doesn't seem to be to blame. If it comes to that, I could have a word with Mr. Banerjee and ask him to reconsider his decision." At the same time, he was not sure if interference in another's affairs was wise unless absolutely necessary. Nevertheless, Uma went back reassured, and with a lightened heart.

The plans of the evening came, unsurprisingly, to nothing the next day. The police wanted to question the servants again, and Bishu and Uma took Priti and their few possessions and walked towards the main road, with its smoke and noise, to catch a bus to Manecktala. Priti looked curiously around her; she thought it was merely an outing. At the bus stop, Bishu said: "After I leaves you at Manecktala, I goes to see Mejda"; Uma seemed not to have heard. Today, before leaving, no goodbyes had been said to the other servants; only the money was collected from Mr. Banerjee and a signature written inside a notebook. "We're going, dadababu," said Bishu, and Mr. Banerjee said: "Keep well." It was a journey from the centre of the city, Ballygunge, with its tall buildings and shops, to what was much farther away and older. The room in the outhouse had not been much, but it had been something in an area where even the rich cannot afford houses; it had given Bishu and Uma a place to stay in proximity to the lives of the well-off, to employment, and yet given them the independence for the life of their small and new family. Now that phase of their lives, which, after all, was so relatively brief that they had hardly become used to it, was ending, and another was about to begin.

Beyond Translation

THE DAKKHINEE BOOKSHOP, at the turning of Lansdowne Road and Rashbehari Avenue—it was really no more
than a pavement bookstall. It stands even now, though with
more than half its books gone, still doing business, but a shadow
of its former self. Yet if you go down Rashbehari Avenue towards
Lake Market in the evening, you can still see it, a series of cup-
boards against a wall, lit by an electric light, and books leaning
against one another upon bookshelves behind their glass-paned
doors; a wonderful bookshelf, exposed to the surrounding pavement and the traffic, as if the house around it had uncannily disappeared.

When I was a boy, and a visitor to Calcutta and my cousins'
house, this was the main bookshop in the area; although it was a
good half hour away from where my cousins lived, we would trek
to it on foot, either with one another, or with our parents and

aunts, on certain days. Any passing car at that time and that year would have seen three boys there, their backs to the road, their heads bent.

Then we would return home with the books in our hands, adventure annuals and mystery stories, my book an English one, and my cousins' books in Bengali. Childhood was a time when I read nothing in Bengali, and my cousins nothing in English; yet none of us really needed to encroach on the others' territory, so rich was the store of children's literature in both languages. Sitting side by side, we would begin to read almost immediately, enveloped in the same contentment as we read our books in different languages, inhabiting different imaginary worlds.

As we read, the routines of the house continued around us. For instance, the maid might be swabbing the floor and the stairs, leaving dark arcs on the red stone. How swift and anonymous and habitual was her task, almost as if a ghost had done it, leaving those dark, moist marks on the floor, which dried and disappeared soon after! Downstairs, my aunt—my cousins' mother—might be overseeing something in the kitchen, while my uncle might be preparing to have an early lunch before going out to work at his small business.

We sat just anywhere while reading, suspending activity, waiting for the story or the book to finish—on the stairs, against the side of a bed, on the floor. It might be the years of the Naxal uprising outside, with young men drawn into the movement, into the spilling of blood, blood that could not be recovered, and the lane, in which both Naxal and Congress supporters lived in some of the houses, was traumatised by those years. Cries would be heard; bottles broken; far away, the explosion of a homemade device. My uncle did not know what to make of this; with his shawl wrapped around his kurta, he was both voluble and innocent; he had always supported the Marxists, but now this was destroying his business, and would drive him to the verge of bankruptcy. Then the years passed. And we still sat reading side by side, of worlds that could not be translated into each other; the changes around us came to us as sounds in the street and from downstairs, that were adornments to our consciousness.

My uncle's business never took off; it was a failure from the start. But optimism never flagged, either. Sometimes, my aunt would come upstairs while we read, perhaps to rearrange something—a pillow on the bed—or to have her bath and do her puja, or to call us downstairs for food. I would be reading about lighthouses, boating adventures, mountain expeditions, while my cousins read about mad scientists and mysteries that Hemendra Kumar Ray had created, about holy men and the seven seas and bloodthirsty kings. Every paisa my aunt spent had to be counted; but they—my uncle and aunt—had great reserves of hospitality and tolerance, so that their worries and struggles never marked their behaviour.

My aunt—whom I will call Shobha mami—hovered around as we sat with our books in our hands; her presence brought us comfort while our minds raced with demons, usurped kingdoms, seashores, and collapsing houses. She was one of those people who have a gift with children, who draw an enchantment around them without any seeming effort; and the spell lasts all childhood. On growing up, I have not come any closer to her; it is almost as if she became someone else; and this is so, most probably, because I knew her as a child. Then, her flaws, her human failings, and the complexity of her character were concealed from me: she appeared to me as a myth would. It was partly, of course, that she was in the midst of her life's beginning; only nine or ten years married, her life had still not closed into a pattern. It was not that she touched or held or kissed us. Her magic and contact were more subtle; she would sort out fish bones for us from a difficult fish; she would tease and joke with us; she would return home, flushed from the market. And she would treat us all alike; not as if we were, all three of us, her sons, but as if we were infinitely and equally interesting. It strikes me now how little I know her, or knew of her desires, fears, affections; but she cannot have been wholly an enigma; it is said that children sometimes see a side of a person that others do not, and if so, we saw a side of her that even she might not have been entirely conscious of.

They were hospitable people; and, in spite of their various burdens during that difficult time, relatives from other parts of the country were always staying with them as students, or visitors (as I was), or as those who were passing through the city. Downstairs there lived for many years an older cousin, brilliant student, son of a widowed aunt, who had left his house in Assam to study in Calcutta and was a mere twelve or thirteen years older than us, and thus almost a contemporary; he would later become a very rich man in America. From time to time, voices came upstairs, of my aunt, our cousin, my uncle, a discussion between the men, talk of lockouts and debts.

But I never thought of myself as a visitor; and I do not know what my cousins thought, as we finished reading our stories in different languages, and looked up, and became conscious once more of the house, with secret flashlight signals and demons who could grow eight times their size in a minute still in our heads. Once finished, the books lost their interest, but remained precious as material objects, that we would pretend to sell each other as make-believe hawkers. But our worlds, essentially, remained locked to each other; we never read each others' stories, though I admired the covers of their books, with severed heads dripping blood, and dragonfly-wing-frail princesses. They would never know what it meant to live outside this world, as I did, of magic and small means; and I would never know what it meant to grow up reading those stories by Saradindu and Sukumar Ray and Hemendra Kumar, and to be transported, for that half hour, more completely into another world, as I believed, than I was.

The Great Game

IT WAS INHUMAN to play cricket at this time of the year, in this heat, but that was precisely what they were doing these days. Moreover, the team was being sent out into that cauldron to pick up something called the Pepsi Cup. You had to feel for them, though they looked like young braves. While others might shop at the airport in Dubai, one would expect *them* not to glance at the watches and shapely state-of-the-art CD players, to have nothing but a glass of orange juice at the hotel before going into the nets.

Among them was Tendulkar, whose name, everyone agreed, sounded like an ancient weapon of destruction, and who carried a one-and-a-half-ton bat. He disembarked from the plane with a singleness of purpose, and a sealed, expressionless face. He and the "boys" (though you wouldn't ordinarily call Azharuddin a "boy") were here to deal with the English and the vigorous Pakistanis, mainly the Pakistanis, who came from a country that had sprung troublingly from a gash in the side of their own about fifty years ago.

Among the spectators was to be Ummar Aziz, who had no place to hide in India and who, rumour had it, had been living around here in a mansion with a swimming pool for the last three years. He had expertly orchestrated a series of explosions in Bombay in 1993, bombs that had gone off in the Air India Building and in Prabhadevi, not to speak of eleven other places. He strenuously denied it, but from this safe haven; and indeed the charge might be a fiction dreamed up by the police. It was heard that he was coming not so much because of his love of cricket, which was considerable, or of the Indian or Pakistani teams (the Pakistani side was a depleted one, with its main bowlers discredited and removed), but because of his fascination with Urmila Deshpande, the star of *Ishq* and *Jaadu,* who was also going to be present. Ummar Aziz had been watching Hindi films since he'd been an orphan child of the Bombay streets.

The team practised nimbly, without exhausting themselves. Now and then a reporter or a television crew came and asked them questions. When Azharuddin answered the questions, you could see the others in the background, throwing their arms about, Tendulkar doing exercises, his glasses so dark they bore no reflection. When he spoke, you had to look at his mouth because of the challenge his dark glasses threw you.

The English were the first to wilt. Ganguly hit the winning shot, a six that saw the ball take flight in a way unlike any bird in these surroundings. Then, the desert sun long set, he got the first Man of the Match award of the tour.

Watching him ascend the crowded podium on a small Sony television, and talk with some assurance, Khatau, who'd just returned from a hard day in the tenements in South Bombay, commented to his colleague Mohammed Yusuf that Ummar Aziz didn't seem to have come to watch the game.

"He certainly wasn't in the crowd; otherwise they would have shown him." Khatau and Mohammed Yusuf were police-men who regretted the way Aziz had, one day, slipped like sand through their fingers. All those explosions; they hadn't been able to do anything about it. Here they were four years later, on their sofas, watching Ganguly under the floodlights.

"Arrey, he won't go to these small-fry games," Yusuf said, shaking his head slowly and with great conviction, while looking at an English player waiting tentatively in the background. Gan-guly was shaking hands with Ravi Shastri. Yusuf wasn't looking at them but staring at the screen and thinking. "He'll come to the big one," he concluded; or words to that effect.

The "big one" was still a few days away, however, days and nights away that is, because they were all "day and night" games, inducing a degree of sleeplessness in the spectator. Before then there was Pakistan versus India, or India versus Pakistan (whichever way you decided to think of it), and Pakistan versus England. After that England would take the first flight out to Heathrow, leaving the battleground open to the warring cousins.

The next day Mita Reddy, former Miss India and runner-up Miss Universe, who had only last year surprised everyone by say-ing to a panel of judges that her favourite person was Mrs. Gandhi—"Indira Gandhi?" "No, Kasturbabai Gandhi," embar-rassing all by invoking the Mahatma's small, self-effacing, long dead wife—was seen in the stands, sitting next to Marshneill Gavaskar, grinning because she could see herself on television. She smiled; and waved—at whom, no one, among the millions watching, knew.

During the thirty-fifth over, by which time seven wickets had fallen for 126 runs, and an Indian medium-pacer and an all-

rounder were putting up an obdurate partnership, there was a
spell of inactivity that sometimes occurs in the middle of an
over, when members of both teams suddenly forget the thou-
sands in the stadium and the TV cameras, and behave like a
family inside a house, unaware they're being watched. Tony
Greig and a minor English ex-bowler were sitting in the com-
mentator's box and discussing plans and strategies, while the little microphone in one of the stumps, placed there to detect the
sound of a nick, eavesdropped on two players conversing:

"Lagta hai woh Aziz kal ayegaa."

Greig was too busy composing a litany about Aussie spin-
bowling, even if he'd known any Hindi, to register anything;
but Khatau, on his sofa, heard the comment, though at first he
wasn't quite sure he had. Yusuf confirmed with a nod that he'd
heard it, too. They hadn't realised that they had an informant in
the middle-stump microphone on the pitch; but then the game
started again. Someone had said Aziz would come tomorrow;
they couldn't be sure if it was one of the Indians, or a Pakistani,
or one of the Indians passing on the information to a Pakistani,
or vice versa. Any of these alternatives might be the right one.

"Fantastic shot," said Yusuf, as Srinath belted an unexpected
cover drive.

Then the camera moved to a tall and swarthy Ravi Shastri,
his cricketing days long over, but finding himself in the midst of
a commentary renaissance, a tie knotted round his neck, laughing and talking to Anju Mahindra, who had once almost married
Rajesh Khanna and gone out with Sir Garfield Sobers. She was
past her heyday; even the long-distance lens couldn't conceal
the tiredness beneath her eyes; she looked abstracted as she listened to Ravi Shastri.

"Is that what they get paid for, yaar?" asked Khatau, reaching
for his beer.

"God it must be hot over there," said Yusuf.

But, contrary to what the microphone in the stump had told them, there was no Aziz the next day, and neither had the more raucous Pakistani supporters, with their shining green flags, come; were they not interested in watching England lose? The Bombay "glitterati" were there again, dutifully, the executive vice president of Pepsi sitting next to the chairman of the Board of Cricket Control in his dark glasses, their wives, in their flaming saris which might have received interrogatory looks from passersby in the streets outside, smiling vacantly at the camera as they stared back at their friends in Bombay, to all appearances unmoved by the hot desert breath. Their children, in striped T-shirts and shorts or jeans, either leaned and lolled against their fathers or revolved like satellites around their parents and parents' friends, tripping lightly down the steps.

Rashid Latif hit the winning runs, and a cry rang out in the stadium. A beautiful woman in a salwaar kameez clapped emphatically.

For the "big one" the stadium was full again. Pakistanis jostled one another; and Indians jostled Pakistanis; and here and there, sheikhs, cell phones in their hands, deshabille, in small, male harems, looked around them, listening to the roar. Boycott knelt in his pressed trousers and short-sleeved shirt and felt the pitch with an arcane hesitation again and again. It was like a dry piece of land, a bit of Arabia, that had never been rained on. He patted it one last time and said to the camera: "Yes, Rahvi, the pitch is flat and true, and there will be runs in it"—as if "runs" were some sort of seed that would sprout shortly, and unexpectedly, from the barren soil.

Mrs. Shweta Kapoor, wife of the relatively recently appointed CEO of Britannia India, was sitting not far from Urmila Deshpande, whom she didn't know, but whose last film, *Jaadu*—"Magic"—she'd seen twice already. The Pakistanis won the toss, elected to bat, and every time Saeed Anwar executed the pull shot, the camera panned to the celebrating Pakistanis and the studiedly sceptical faces of the Indians, and also to Shweta Kapoor, who'd once been a newsreader, a personality in her own right, and to her husband, whose youthful face was overhung by prematurely greying hair, and then to Urmila Deshpande, who was inscrutable and indecipherable behind her dark glasses. There was a rumour, uncorroborated, that she was seeing Jadeja, who was standing hunched, not far away, at mid-off.

The previous day, both Mrs. Kapoor and Urmila Deshpande had had their hair done at the Hilton; Urmila had acquired the permanent curls she'd need for a film once she got back. Mrs. Kapoor had bought a portable CD player, with a three-CD changer, for her son. The camera now discovered a group of men in the cheaper stalls who were holding up a placard: HI URMILA YOU HAVE DONE JAADU TO OUR HEARTS. The moment they realised they were on television, the sign began to vibrate as if it were alive in their hands. The next minute Ijaz Ahmed was out to a catch at gully held by Azharuddin. The camera showed Mrs. Kapoor smiling and saying something to a beautiful woman next to her, as if exchanging a particularly unworthy piece of gossip; and then it showed a young man clapping, fair, with blond hair, colourless eyes, who could have passed for a European but for the fullness of his lips.

"They're all there," said Inspector Khatau, sucking in his stomach.

"Who's he—never heard of him?" Yusuf asked with justifiable irritation.

Raghav Chopra had displayed his latest collection only two weeks ago at the Taj: cholis, twenty-first-century ghagras; "Clothes are a language that changes before other languages do," he'd said in an interview. Mita Reddy had been one of the models. In her column, Mita Reddy had been christened "a dark Kate Moss" by Shobha De, a "will-o'-the-wisp."

"Where is Sharjah?" asked Khatau finally.

"I don't know," said Yusuf, looking blank. "Near Du-Dubai." He added, "That guy doesn't look *Indian*, yaar!"

As far as everyone knew, though, Raghav Chopra was a real blond. How he'd come to be one was a mystery no one enquired into. The colour of the hair had changed probably as the universe had changed temperature; just as orange frogs were found recently in English gardens.

"Three hundred and five," said Khatau, rising suddenly. "Phew!"

All out, 305 runs. Boycott proclaimed that defeat was at hand.

"It's a known fact," he said, "that Eendiuns are no good at chasing!" He shook his head and seemed to smile in bewilderment at his words. Floodlights had been switched on about an hour ago, night had come and brought with it a school of dragonflies cruising through the field. The saris were lit up, and the women moved uncomfortably. The desert sky was like a great, empty theatre.

Twenty minutes later, Tendulkar came out with his heavy bat in one hand, followed by the taller, shuffling Ganguly. The camera noted two people in deep conversation, but it was impossible to hear what they were saying.

"Sachin's our secret weapon," observed one of them, a gentlewoman who lived on Malabar Hill in a flat overlooking Kamala Nehru Park.

"And not Trishul or any of the other warheads?" said her husband's colleague. She smiled politely and refused to indicate that she'd understood, then fanned herself gently with a magazine.

As Aquib Javed bowled the first ball, the crowd's voice swelled in a hum and then subsided again. On the television screen, Tendulkar's bat, its face as remorseless as its staunch owner's, descended straight on the ball and hit it onto the ground. A deep thud, magnified by the microphone in the stump, accompanied this event.

"Hey! Hey!" said Khatau. "Look, bhai."

The camera had come to rest, in innocence, on the face of a man scratching his cheek.

"It's our man, bhai! It's our bridegroom, who left at the wedding!"

The camera now withdrew prudently to a safer place, a minor and timid crook in a nasty area. Then, panning from a group of agitated men holding up a sign saying TON-dulkar, it framed the man who'd been scratching his cheek thoughtfully moments earlier, sitting next to the chairman of the Board of Cricket Control and his wife and, a few seats to the right, Urmila Deshpande, who seemed absorbed in the course of the match.

"Saala!" said Yusuf; and his mouth remained open.

"Don't abuse your brother-in-law," said Khatau, but he didn't feel like laughing.

The man who'd almost blown up Bombay, who'd had bombs placed in Nariman Point and Dadar and eleven other places, had taken care to wear a pale, pressed green shirt, and had probably had a haircut; he now took out a cell phone. With excessive politeness, he spoke a few words into the receiver. His face, when in close-up, revealed a ravaged and uneven skin.

THERE WERE sixty runs on the board, forty-six of them made by Tendulkar off fifty balls, when the sky darkened. The weather reports had made no predictions; the batsmen looked up at what little they could see of the sky. The floodlights dimmed.

"Oh dear, oh dear, it seems like a dooststorm," said Boycott.

The women in the expensive seats looked uneasy; their husbands laughed in their suits and belligerently talked business with one another. A man leaned forward and said something in Ummar Aziz's ear. Tony Greig and Gavaskar initiated a detailed discussion of the match so far, and replays of a brighter time, when batsmen had played their shots in the light of day, began to be shown.

"Chai lau?" said a ten-year-old boy in shorts.

"No, idiot," said Khatau. "What, tea at this time of the night?" Reprimanded, the boy sat down quietly, and gratefully, on the floor before the television.

Every time the camera returned to the ground, it showed the dust swirling in minute particles across it. Tendulkar was still wearing his protective headgear, boiling in the dressing room, staring back hard at the night; yet, in the prolific commercial breaks, there he was again, leaning against a van and drinking Pepsi-Cola, or wearing a striped T-shirt and flashing a Visa card. Meanwhile, the Bombay housewives pressed saris against their faces and looked for a moment like local Muslim women; but Urmila Deshpande's face remained composed, as if nothing had happened. Again and again, the commentators scrutinised a slow-motion almost-run-out from the afternoon, Saeed Anwar raising his bat and setting out infinitesimally on his long odyssey, while Ijaz Ahmed, too, in agonising protractedness, lunged towards the white line.

When play resumed an hour later, Tendulkar came back looking intent; at the other end, Ganguly began to prod the ball gently and sent it to somewhere near the boundary. Raghav Chopra ran his hand through his hair; it looked absolutely white in the floodlights. The women from Bombay self-consciously dusted their saris.

"If there's anyone who can win India the match," said Ravi Shastri in his oratorial voice, "it's that man out there." For no one referred to Tendulkar by name anymore.

"He's gone," said Khatau, despondent.

Ummar Aziz had disappeared; Khatau had been absorbing this fact for the last five minutes. Urmila had gone as well, probably to a different destination, but he couldn't help noticing it. The one nondescript and aging, the other resplendent. "Beauty and the Beast," thought Khatau in bold letters.

Almost immediately, Tendulkar, on sixty-one, was bowled by an in-swinger. One large section of the crowd—the Indians—stared into the distance, as if a film they'd been watching had been stopped midway. The others danced festively, as if a country separated them from the Indians.

"How did that happen," enquired Boycott, "to the little master?"

The executive vice president of Pepsi moved impatiently in his seat; he'd been talking to his companion about a rival bid from Coke at that moment. Tendulkar, his head bowed beneath his visor, strode heavily towards the pavilion; but, almost immediately, he was drinking Pepsi, leaning against a van, and flashing a Visa card ("Now You Go Get It"), indifferent to his debacle.

"But how did you know, yaar?" said Yusuf, curving the palm of his hand in a question.

"What?" asked Khatau, straightening his shirt.

"You said just now, 'He's gone.' How did you know he's going to be out?" Yusuf smiled. "You're a clairvoyant or what?"

The dismissal was shown twice from the point of view of the stump camera: the ball rising from near the batsman's feet, so quickly as almost to hit Khatau's and Yusuf's faces, and then the lens falling backward and staring lidlessly at the sky, a dead eye gazing at space.

In spite of the floodlights, the Indians in the stadium could see only darkness about them. It was left to Ganguly and Jadeja, throwing huge and fluent shadows, to build up a partnership of two hundred runs and steer the side to an unlikely victory. Anju Mahindra, who half an hour ago had been exhausted, now looked rejuvenated and fifteen years younger, and waved at someone who was presumably still awake in Bombay. Jadeja leaned forward and hit the winning four; on another channel Urmila Deshpande, her hair long and with no curls in it, sang sweet, tuneless words to Salmaan Khan upon a beach.

At one o'clock in the morning, a loud celebratory firecracker went off in Bandra. Khatau shuddered at the noise of the explosion, and thought of Ummar Aziz, small, nondescript, scratching his cheek thoughtfully.

Real Time

ON THEIR WAY to the house, Mr. Mitra said he didn't know if they should buy flowers. They were very near Jogu Bazaar; and Mr. Mitra suddenly raised one hand and said:

"Abdul, slowly!"

The driver eased the pressure on the accelerator and brought the Ambassador almost to a standstill. Not looking into the rearview mirror, he studied two boys with baskets playing on the pavement on his left.

"Well, what should we do?" Mr. Mitra's face, as he turned to look at his wife, was pained, as if he was annoyed she hadn't immediately come up with the answer.

"Do what you want to do quickly," she said, dabbing her cheek with her sari. "We're already late." She looked at the small dial of her watch. He sighed; his wife never satisfied him when he needed her most; and quite probably it was the same story the other way round. Abdul, who, by sitting on the front seat, claimed to be removed to a sphere too distant for the words at the back to be audible, continued to stare at the children while keeping the engine running.

"But I'm not sure," said the husband, like a distraught child, "given the circumstances."

She spoke then in a voice of sanity she chose to speak in only occasionally.

"Do what you'd do in a normal case of bereavement," she said. "This is no different."

He was relieved at her answer, but regretted that he had to go out of the car into the market. He was wearing a white cotton shirt and terycotton trousers because of the heat, and shoes; he now regretted the shoes. He remembered he hadn't been able to find his sandals in the cupboard. His feet, swathed in socks, were perspiring.

He came back after about ten minutes, holding half a dozen tuberoses against his chest, cradling them with one arm; a boy was running after him. "Babu, should I wipe the car, should I wipe the car . . . ," he was saying, and Mr. Mitra looked intent, like a man who has an appointment. He didn't acknowledge the boy; inside the car, Mrs. Mitra, who was used to these inescapable periods of waiting, moved a little. He placed the tuberoses in the front, next to Abdul, where they smeared the seat with their moisture. Mr. Mitra had wasted some time bargaining, bringing down the price from sixteen to fourteen rupees, after which the vendor had expertly tied a thread round the lower half of the flowers.

"Why did she do it?" he asked in an offhand way, as the car proceeded once more on its way. Going down Ashutosh Mukherjee Road, they turned left into Southern Avenue.

Naturally, they didn't have the answer. They passed an apartment building they knew, Shanti Nivas, its windows open but dark and remote. Probably they'd been a little harsh with her, her parents. Her marriage, sixteen years ago, had been seen to be appropriate. Usually, it's said, Lakshmi, the goddess of wealth, and Saraswati, of learning, two sisters, don't bless the same house; but certainly that wasn't true of the Poddars, who had two bars-at-law in the generation preceding this one, and a social reformer in the lineage, and also a white four-storeyed mansion on a property near Salt Lake where they used to have garden parties. Anjali had married Gautam Poddar very soon after taking her M.A. in history from Calcutta University.

As they passed a petrol pump, Mr. Mitra wondered what view traditional theology took of this matter, and how the rites accommodated an event such as this—she had jumped from a third-floor balcony—which couldn't, after all, be altogether uncommon. Perhaps there was no ceremony. In his mind's eye, when he tried to imagine the priest, or the long rows of tables at which people were fed, he saw a blank. But Abdul couldn't identify the lane.

"Bhai, is this Rai Bahadur R.C. Mullick Road?" he asked a loiterer somewhat contemptuously.

The man leaned into a window and looked with interest at the couple in the back, as if unwilling to forgo this opportunity to view Mr. and Mrs. Mitra. Then, examining the driver's face again, he pointed to a lane before them, going off to the right, next to a sari shop that was closed.

"That one there."

They went down for about five minutes, past two-storeyed houses with small but spacious courtyards, each quite unlike the others, till they had to stop again and ask an adolescent standing by a gate where Nishant Apartments was. The boy scratched his arm and claimed there was no such place over here. As they looked at him disbelievingly, he said, "It may be on *that* side," pointing to the direction they'd just come from.

"That side?" Mr. Mitra looked helpless; he'd given up trying to arrive on time. What preoccupied him now was not getting there, but the negotiations involved in how to get there.

It turned out that what the boy was suggesting was simple. The main road, Lansdowne Road, divided the two halves of Rai Bahadur Mullick Road; one half of Mullick Road went left, the other right.

"Don't you know where they live?" asked Mr. Mitra as Abdul reversed and turned the car around. The over-sweet, reminiscent smell of the tuberoses rose in the front of the car with a breeze that had come unexpectedly through the window. In front of a house on the left, clothes hung to dry as a child went round and round in circles in the courtyard on a tricycle.

"But I've only been there three or four times—and the last time, two years ago!" she complained. "I find these lanes so confusing."

The lanes *were* confusing; there were at least two, one after another, that looked exactly the same, with their clotheslines, grilles, and courtyards.

About ten or eleven days ago, they'd noticed a small item in the newspaper, and were shocked to recognise who it was. Then an obituary appeared, and Mr. Mitra had called his daughter in Delhi, who remembered Anjali from visits made in childhood. Last week another insertion had told them that "Observances will be made in memory of Mrs. Anjali Poddar, who passed away on the 23rd of February, at 11 A.M. at 49 Nishant Apartments, Rai Bahadur R.C. Mullick Road. All are welcome."

They didn't expect it would be a proper shraddh ceremony; they didn't think people would be fed. So Mrs. Mitra had told the boy at home, firmly so as to impress her words upon him, "We'll be back by one o'clock! Cook the rice and keep the daal and fish ready!" Without mentioning it clearly, they'd decided they must go to the club afterwards to get some cookies for tea, and stop at New Market on the way back. So they must leave the place soon after twelve; it was already ten past eleven.

The first to be fed was usually a crow, for whom a small ball of kneaded aata was kept on the balcony for it to pick up; the crow was supposed to be the soul come back—such absurd make-believe! Yet everyone did it, as if it were some sort of nursery game. Mr. Mitra, looking out through the windshield, past the steering wheel and Abdul's shoulder, speculated if such practices might be all right in this case. Here the soul had made its own exit, and it was difficult to imagine why it would want to come back to the third-floor balcony of Nishant Apartments.

"Ask him!" said Mrs. Mitra, prodding her husband's arm with a finger. She nodded towards a watchman standing in front of what looked like a bungalow. "Ask him!"

"Nishant?" said the thin, moustached chowkidar, refusing to get up from his stool. Behind him was an incongruously large bungalow, belonging to a businessman, hidden by an imposing white gate and a wall. He barely allowed himself a smile. "But there it is." Two houses away, on the left.

It was clear from the size of the cramped compound, with the ceiling overhanging the porch only a few feet away from the adjoining wall, that Nishant had been erected where some older house once was, and which had been sold off to property developers and contractors. It must be twelve or thirteen years old. An Ambassador and two Marutis were parked outside by the pavement. Mr. Mitra, holding the tuberoses under his right arm, glanced at his watch as he entered the porch, then got into the lift, which had a collapsible gate, hesitantly. He waited for his wife, looked at himself quickly in the mirror, and pressed a button. Mrs. Mitra smoothed her hair and looked at the floors changing through the collapsible gate.

A narrow, tiled, clean corridor, going past forty-six and forty-seven, led to the main door to forty-nine, which was open. Faint music emanated to the corridor, and a few people could be seen moving about in the hall. There was a jumble of slippers and sandals and shoes by the door, promiscuously heaped on one another. Mr. Mitra took off his with an impatient movement; Mrs. Mitra descended delicately from hers—they had small, two-inch heels.

Mr. Talukdar, who was standing in a white shirt and trousers talking to another couple and a man, excused himself from their company and came to the newly arrived couple. "Come in, come in," he said to Mrs. Mitra. To Mr. Mitra he said nothing, but accepted the tuberoses that were now transferred to his arms. "Nilima's there," he said, indicating a woman who was sitting at the far side of the sitting room upon a mattress on the floor, an old woman near her. So saying, he went off slowly with the tuberoses in another direction.

A small crystal chandelier hung from the ceiling, gleaming in daylight. Near where Nilima, Anjali's mother, sat, a ceiling fan turned slowly. Some of the furniture had been cleared away for mats to be laid out on the floor, but some, including two armchairs and a divan, had been left where they were. On the sideboard was a Mickey Mouse–shaped pencil box, next to a few photographs and curios. A clock upon one of the shelves said it was eleven-twenty-five.

Mr. Talukdar was a tallish man, heavy, fair, clean-shaven. Most of his hair was grey, and thinning slightly. He'd held some sort of important position in an old British industrial company that had turned into a large public-sector concern a decade after independence: British Steel, renamed National Steel. He was now standing next to a television set, whose convex screen was dusty, and talking to someone.

Mr. Mitra seemed to remember that Mr. Talukdar had two sons in America, and that the sons had children. But Anjali had

had no children, and that might have made things worse for her. He looked at a man singing a Brahmo sangeet on a harmonium in the middle of the room, attended by only a few listeners, and saw that it was someone he knew, an engineer at Larsen & Toubro.

The song stopped, and the sound of groups of people talking became more audible. The hubbub common to shraddh ceremonies was absent: people welcoming others as they came in, even the sense, and the conciliatory looks, of bereavement. Instead there was a sort of pointlessness, as people refused to acknowledge what did not quite have a definition. Mr. Mitra's stomach growled.

He looked at his wife in the distance, the bun of hair prominent at the back of her head; she bent and said something to Nilima, Anjali's mother. Suddenly there was a soft, whining sound that repeated itself, low but audible; it was the cordless phone. Mr. Talukdar stooped to pick it up from a chair and, distractedly looking out of the window, said "Hello" into the receiver, and then more words, nodding his head vigorously once, and gesturing with his hand. He walked a few steps with the cordless against his ear, gravitating towards a different group of people. Mr. Mitra realised that the tuberoses he'd brought had been placed on that side of the room, beside three or four other bouquets.

He felt bored; and he noticed a few others, too, some of whom he knew, looking out of place. Shraddh ceremonies weren't right without their mixture of convivial pleasure and grief; and he couldn't feel anything as complete as grief. He'd known Anjali slightly; how well do you know your wife's distant relations, after all? He'd known more about her academic record, one or two charming anecdotes to do with her success at school, her decent first-class degree, and about her husband,

Gautam Poddar, diversifying into new areas of business, than about her.

"Saab?"

Thank God! A man was standing before him with a platter of sandesh—he picked up one; it was small and soft; he took a tiny bite. It must be from Banchharam or Nepal Sweets; it had that texture. There was another man a little farther away, with a tray of Fanta and Coca-Cola. Mr. Mitra hesitated for a second and then walked towards the man. He groped for a bottle that was less cold than the others; he had a sore throat developing.

"Mr. Mitra!"

There was a man smiling widely at him, a half-empty Coke bottle with a straw in one hand.

"I hope you remember me; or do I need to introduce my-self?"

"No, I don't remember you; but I spoke to someone at the club just the other day who looks very like you, a Mr. Amiya Sar-badhikari," said Mr. Mitra jovially, taking a sip of faintly chilled Fanta. A large painting of a middle-aged woman holding flowers faced them.

They talked equably of recent changes in their companies, catching up from where they'd left it in their last exchange; then to their children, and a brief disagreement about whether civil engineering had a future as a career today.

"Oh, I think so," said Mr. Sarbadhikari, "certainly in the de-veloping world, in the Middle East, if not in the West." His Coke bottle was now almost empty; he held it symbolically, put-ting off finishing the dregs to a moment later. There was an un-easiness in their conversation, though, as if they were avoiding something; it was their being here they were avoiding. Of course, people never remembered the dead at shraddh cere-monies; they talked about other things; but that forgetfulness occurred effortlessly. In this case, the avoidance was strategic and self-conscious; the conversation tripped from subject to subject.

"Mr. Mitra, all this Coke has swollen my bladder," said Sarbadhikari suddenly, "and, actually, from the moment I stepped in . . ."

From his manner it looked like he was familiar with Talukdar's flat. Gathering the folds of his dhuti in one hand, he turned histrionically and padded off in the direction of a bathroom door. A child, the only one among the people who'd come, ran from one end of the hall to the other. There were a few people on the balcony; Mr. Mitra decided to join them.

"I told them," a woman was saying to a companion, "this is no way to run a shop; if you don't exchange a purchase, say so, but don't sell damaged goods."

He quietly put down the bottle of Fanta on the floor. There wasn't much of a view; there was the wall, which ran towards the street you couldn't see, and another five-storeyed building with little, pretty balconies. Below him was the porch to the left, and the driveway, which seemed quite close. A young woman, clearly not a maidservant, was hanging towels from the railing in one of the balconies opposite.

Did it happen here? He looked at the woman attach clips to another towel. Apparently those who always threaten to, don't. Anjali had been living with her parents for a month after leaving her husband. She'd left him before, but this time she'd said her intentions were clear and final. There was a rumour that her parents had not been altogether sympathetic, and had been somewhat obtuse; but it's easy to be lucid with hindsight. He was still hungry, and he looked back into the hall to see if he could spot the man with the sandesh. But he had temporarily disappeared. As he moved about exploratorily, he caught his wife's eye and nodded at her as if to say, Yes, I'm coming, and, Yes, it's been a waste of time.

Cautiously, he tried to trace, from memory, the route that he'd seen Sarbadhikari take about ten minutes ago. He found himself in a bedroom where the double bed had been covered neatly with a pink bedcover; he coughed loudly. He opened a door to what might be the bathroom and, once inside, closed it behind him again. As he urinated into the commode, he studied a box, printed with flowers, of Odomos room freshener kept above it; then he shivered involuntarily, and shrugged his shoulders. He had a vaguely unsatisfying feeling, as if the last half hour had lacked definition.

Once inside the car, he said to his wife, "I don't know about you, but I'm quite ravenous."

Prelude to an Autobiography: A Fragment

I FELT THE URGE to write this after I began to read Shobha De's memoirs. If she can write her memoir, I thought, so can I. For who would have thought, Shobha De least of all, that one day she would write her life story for other people to read? She had been an ordinary, if beautiful, girl who got recruited (as she says) from a middle-class home into modelling, never particularly interested in studies (I was the same at her age), and then, through accident and ambition, got married into one of Bombay's richest families, started her own magazine and began writing her own gossip column, got divorced, reinvented herself as a writer of middles for Bombay newspapers, married again, became India's first successful pulp novelist, and now has written her memoirs. Through what a strange chain of events people arrive at the world of writing—and Shobha De's tranformation has been one of the most unexpected in my lifetime. It shows me the endless possibilities of the society we have lived in. And I ask myself the question: if she can be a writer, and inscribe her thoughts and impressions in language, why not I?

There's the question, of course, of who would want to read my memoirs, or whatever it is I'm setting out to write—because I'm not altogether sure what it is. But (although I've never seen myself as a writer before) these are questions, I'm certain, that preoccupy (inasmuch as I can enter the mind of a writer) all who write (it's an area I know little about). And it consoles me to think that at one time every writer must have done what I'm doing now, starting out and not knowing where it was leading to. It's not a feeling you can communicate to someone who's never tried it. Some people, I'm sure, end up taking this route by intention and dedication, after years of preparation—my daughter has a friend who, at thirteen, is already writing lovely poems that have been published in *Femina* and her school magazine; I'm sure she'll be a fine writer one day, and she looks set for that course. Others, like myself, and probably Shobha De, arrive at that route by chance (although Shobha De very differently from me), and it's from her that I take a kind of courage, that she should have ended up a writer, although it makes me smile even as I say it.

Yet I'm not quite sure of my English, though it's the only language I have. My knowledge of the Indian languages is passing; I can speak a smattering of a few, but can't read or write any one of them with authority. I was born in Patna, of a Gujarati mother and a father who is a deracinated Andhra Brahmin; my link to any Indian language became, thus, tenuous. I'm not sure who'd be interested in any of this, though; why should anyone want to know why I write in English, or who my parents were, or how they came to be my parents? But I take heart from small things, besides the uncontrollable urge to get on with the job at hand, an urge that I don't quite understand; "small things" like the fact that a new writer comes into being almost every day. This is terrifying, but it also gives me (and, I'm sure, many others like me) the impetus to take the first step. I don't necessarily admire all the writers around me, but sometimes it is good to have their presences about (many of them will not be heard of again) as I start out on this venture.

MY HUSBAND CAME IN a little earlier from the office yesterday than he usually does, energetic but starved, and he caught me sitting alone, looking out at the sea. "What are you doing?" he asked quizzically; and I started. I think I looked guilty. I knew we had a party to go to in the evening. How could I tell him that I was trying to do something I became ashamed of the moment he entered, that I was trying to frame a sentence?

I WENT TO a Christian school, and learnt to speak the words of the Lord's Prayer before I knew what they were. This was in the hot hall of my convent in Patna, with a few hundred other girls, only a few of whose names I remember. I mumbled the words without knowing what they were, and never have found out; but I spoke them reverentially and grew up believing in God. Whenever I thought of a Supreme Deity, which was not often but not altogether infrequently, either, it was God I thought of, rather than "parameshwar" or "ishwar." But I have never been inside a church, except as a tourist in Goa.

My father's beliefs were contradictory; that is, his beliefs about religion. His beliefs were to do with human beings, the future of the country, and, most important, the upbringing of children. Children must be given love and pride of place, but career must be given priority, too, for the opportunities it will provide, eventually, one's children. God he hardly mentioned at all, except during the crises in his career, when he would mention him philosophically rather than religiously, saying, for instance, "Well, no one can change what God has already determined." When I write these words about him, I feel I'm not only describing my father but a general figure, someone whom many other people will recognise in their father. Mothers and fathers belong half to fiction, anyway; it's not as if you're only their biological offspring; they, too, have reinvented themselves as parents to give you, while you live, the fiction of themselves.

WHOM DOES ONE write for? At least one of the answers will have to be—"David Davidar." When I do put my thoughts in order, when I do finally set out on this project, it's him I shall be thinking of. Because he gives me, and others like me, a valid reason. It gives us hope that someone will rescue our manuscripts, our thoughts put down and carefully typed on paper, from oblivion and eternity. Because I am sure that he doesn't—I don't know him, but I have composed him, as an individual with motives and conceptions and almost no prejudices, willy-nilly, piecemeal from what I've read from twenty or thirty articles about writing and publishing over the last eight or nine years— I'm sure he doesn't consign anything to the dustbin until he's given it a proper chance. And Lord knows, he must have quite a few manuscripts upon his table. Not all of them are from famous people. When he came into our lives about ten or eleven years ago (I can't remember exactly when), it was as if he wasn't quite real—we might have dreamed him up. It was as if he'd come from nowhere. But apparently he actually comes from the South; or at least he looks like a South Indian (I've seen him on television). One day—not too far from now, I hope—my manuscript will be waiting at his table.

WHERE TO BEGIN? As I've said to you, the only language I have is English. I remember learning longhand in kindergarten, rows of letters, first a series of a's, then b's, and so on.

I'M UNCOMFORTABLE beginning at the beginning. It's not because I'm clever, but because it's a difficult thing, writing. And I haven't had any past experience. I used to write poems, of course, when I was quite young; they were passionate and formless but somehow arranged themselves into short and long lines and stanzas without my having to do much about it. Later, they stopped altogether. I suppose it was because I became not unattractive and, after an awkward puberty, when I wasn't sure of myself, acquired a circle of friends and a "social life." You will wonder at the inverted commas, but, in the seventies, so much of what we did was in inverted commas; "sex," "love," "going all the way"; we all talked about it, but half of it was conversation and fantasy, we didn't go "all the way."

I THINK THE EARLY YEARS in Patna, though my memories of them are few, and often random and disconnected, must be the reason why I've never felt I belong here—to Bombay— although this is where I grew up. Yet I never think of myself as a person who "comes from Bombay"; it's the place I've lived in much of my life. Where do I come from, then? I don't have to go to Gujarat to visit my Gujarati relatives; many of them live here, on Peddar Road. My nani, my mother's mother, died in a third-

floor flat in a building at the turning of Peddar Road and Ga-
madia Road.

YOU ASK ME if I feel more South Indian or Gujarati—I don't
know. I know a few Telegu words, but my father didn't speak
very much in Telegu at home. The language my parents spoke to
each other was English. I grew up in a fifth-floor apartment on
Nepean Sea Road, very near where the small flyover was built in
the seventies. How many walks my friends, especially Kamini,
who lived in the same building, and I took across that flyover!

Kamini and I, too, spoke to each other in English, although
her parents were from the Andhra as well; but it never occurred
to us to experiment with Telegu in our conversation. I don't think
we even had a clear idea that we were South Indians, I at least in
part; the solidarity we felt had to do with the fact that we went to
the same school. The English we spoke, I now realize, was gar-
nished with Hindi words for effect; it all sounded very clever-
clever: "Didn't do too well in my chemistry paper. Chalta hai,
yaar!" This was our Esperanto, and we never thought to think it
anything but English; it wouldn't have done to speak in any other
kind of English. The girls who spoke in "perfect" English were
slightly ridiculous and were supposed to be "goody-goody."

That's exactly the Esperanto that Shobha De (then Raja-
dhyaksha) and her colleagues began to write in *Stardust* in the
seventies. There was something slightly impolite about that language, wasn't there?—all right for schoolgirls to speak in, but to
write in . . . ?

ALTHOUGH SO MANY PEOPLE write these days (so many, it's
difficult to imagine), you feel the world you know, the India you

know, is still to be written about. Is this merely solipsistic? Shobha (I hope she won't mind me using her first name) has scratched the tip of the iceberg, though; I now feel that her life is also in some way mine—I don't mean the celebrity; though even celebrity emerges from that book, *Selective Memory* (what an apposite, an inevitable name!), as a kind of character, a desirable freak that some people got to know in Bombay at that time, rather than as destiny. Even the portfolio of photographs, the author now with Amitabh Bachchan, or Indira Gandhi, or Nari Hira, looks slightly doctored, as if all the photos of Shobha De had been taken on the same day, for she is the same—perpetually young, her carved face immutable—in all of them, while the others—Nari Hira, Amitabh Bachchan—are fraught with contingency, they look like trespassers. I've seen the tricks that are possible these days; that's why John F. Kennedy looks like an intruder, alone and slightly nervous, when he's made to shake hands in *Forrest Gump* with Tom Hanks without being certain he's in the movie.

But that's not what I mean when I say that Shobha De's life is in some way mine. It's not the celebrity; it's the detritus that we all know but no one speaks of, the banal, briefly glittering sequence of events, where the heart beats underneath. That is what I'm concerned with; because that is when I feel myself in the silence, on the edge of the words, not yet a writer (just as she is not yet a writer) but listening to what we in the upper middle class in Bombay frivolously call "life." Because, however much we insist, we will never be quite writers; literature is not where we start from. All those years, going to the matinee, borrowing books from the British Council, thinking you might be acquiring a boyfriend—literature was not what proscribed or described those episodes. Of course, we read books (I think Shobha did as well), and I even studied English literature; but that was studying other people's lives, authors and characters.

Where our hearts beat, that was secret, or disappointing, or satisfying, or trivial, too trivial for it to become words or a story. Really, our lives were glamorous and happy but too trivial. And it is there that I must begin, that is why all of us writers who have still not written a word are impatient to disturb the silence.

The Second Marriage

ALTHOUGH ONE OF THEM lived in Kensington and the other in Bayswater, they didn't know each other. It was that evening, when he'd come out of the underground and walked down the road glittering with light and rain, and gone back home to speak to his parents on the telephone, that he'd first heard about her. A second marriage! What *was* marriage, after all? The back of his overcoat was velvety with moisture as it lay drying on the sofa, where it had been roughly put aside. Once, after a couple of meetings, it was agreed that the idea of a second marriage was congenial to both of them, they decided to put it to execution. They had no idea, really, what it was all about; members of both sides of the family became like co-conspirators, and decided to keep the fact a secret till they had an inkling as to what the shape and features of a second marriage were. As far as they were concerned, it was still as formless as the rain on Kensington High Street. Last time, the rituals, like some vast fabric whose provenance they knew little about, had woven them into the marriage, without their having to enquire deeply into it; Arun remembered, from long ago, the car that had come to pick him up, his eyes smarting with the smoke from the fire, the web of flowers over everything, including the bed, the stage, even the car. The first marriage had been like a book into which everyone, including they, had been written, melding unconsciously and without resistance into the characters in it that everyone was always supposed to be.

They met at an old pub near Knightsbridge, and ordered two coffees. This time Prajapati, or Brahma, would not preside with wings unfurled from the sky or the dark over their marriage; nor would this wedding be in that ageless lineage that had begun when Shiva had importunately stormed in to marry Parvati. This time the gods would be no more than an invisible presence between their conversation. They sat there, two individuals, rather lonely, both carrying their broken marriages like the rumours of children.

"Sugar?" she said, with the air of one who was conversant with his habits. He was shyer than she was, as if he needed to prove something.

"Two," he said, managing to sound bold and nervous at once.

They were like two film directors who had with them a script, a plan, but nothing else. There was both exhaustion and hope in their eyes and gestures, which the waitress, saying "Thank you!" cheerfully, hadn't noticed.

"Two?" she said, noting that he was overweight. A gentle affection for him had preceded, in her, any permanent bond. It was as if it would almost not matter if they never saw each other again.

"Are you all right?" said the waitress, coming back after a while.

"Oh, we're fine!" he said, his English accent impeccable.

"Maybe you could bring me a few cookies." The cookies were pale star-shaped squiggles, or chocolate-dark circles. They had brought a list of invitees with them.

"This is Bodo Jethu," she said, pointing at the name, "A. Sarkar," on the top of a piece of paper. "You'll see him during the ashirbaad at Calcutta." Withdrawing her finger and looking at a name, she said, "That's my only mama." He stared at the name she was looking at.

Six years ago, these very people, six years younger, had blessed her at the ashirbaad ceremony before her first marriage. Now they would have to be summoned again, like figures brought to life a second time from a wooden panel where they'd been frozen, resurrected from their armchairs, or old-age homes, or holiday resorts, or wherever they happened to be. The embarrassment, the fatigue, of blessing a niece, or a grandniece, or a daughter, a second time! Some of them had developed a few aches and pains, inexorably, since the first time; though all of them were still there. Now they'd be brought back like soldiers that had been disbanded and were caught loitering happily and absently.

But the list of invitees, this time round, was to be a more makeshift affair. It had the air of an impressionistic personal reminiscence; it had been composed, without much advice from elders, haltingly, from memory. "Might as well put *him* there" and "Don't you have anyone else on your father's side of the family?" were the expressions of collaboration and trade heard being made across the coffee cups, smudged with marks from their lips, on the table. Last time, the list of invitees in both cases had been all-encompassing; almost all the people who populated their lives on a long-term basis had come. This time, only a handful were to come; some people had been left out mysteriously, for no good reason; others were the most essential, the kind of people they'd have chosen to take with them to a nuclear-free zone, in case of a war, if they were offered the choice.

In everything they said, there was this air of acceptance and tentative experimentation rather than celebration, of a resolve towards provisionality rather than finality; since they themselves, rather than tradition, authority, or destiny, were having to author this event, they were experiencing the difficulty that authors have, of bringing into existence what didn't exist before. In Arpita, especially, there was a deep sadness, not so much because she was attached to her ex-husband, whom she hated, but because she realised the marriage ceremony has only one incarnation, it has no second birth or afterlife, that the fire cannot be lit again, consumed and charred as it had been by ghee, nor the garlands re-exchanged, except in memory, where it can be played again and again, like a videotape. Whose wedding was that, then, six years ago, and whose wedding was it to be now? There was a subtle disjuncture between meaning and reality. In the meanwhile, they, while considering the idea of the wedding and the marriage, were having to behave like visitors from a remote planet who were studying the civilizations of this one from a book, and finding their habits increasingly difficult to put to use.

Later, after he'd paid the three pounds and fifty—there was a brief discussion about who should have the right to pay, till it was decided that it was not so much a question of rights as of who had the change—they took a tube (both of them had taken the day off from the office) to Highgate, and walked down from there to Hampstead Heath. There were two or three preponderant clouds in the sky, which were being gradually pushed beyond their field of vision by a breeze, but there didn't seem to be any immediate danger of rain. The Heath was largely touristless and deserted except for a few devout ramblers and the usual conference of ducks and a few expatiating, unidentifiable birds that, as they walked, had the strangely private and liberated air of tramps. They went to take a look, from the outside, at the old, stately home where they would have their reception in London—they could well afford it; they each earned more than fifty thousand pounds a year—after the ashirbaad and reception in Calcutta. They were too well dressed to be loiterers or intruders, Arun in his usual overcoat, Arpita in her slacks and her dark blue duffel coat. An onlooker, looking at them looking at the stately home, might have concluded they'd come here to attend a function, only to discover they'd arrived on the wrong day.

"It's lovely, isn't it?" he said, dazzled by the sunlight mutely reflecting on the wooden door.

"It's very nice," she said, nodding. The old two-storeyed house with long verandahs where she'd first been married, a family house converted and rented out for such occasions, had set like a sun, while this one had risen like a new sun which has no name, only an indefinable light, in its place. She couldn't look at it properly. This past month, she couldn't tell clearly if she was happy because she was at last getting married, or because she was getting married in the light of her imperfections, and others'; that imperfection, as much as accomplishment, would define them when bride and bridegroom finally met. This second time round, she'd discovered that to be happy was not so much a self-sufficient, spontaneous emotion, such as you might feel in relation to a dream or a secret, but a way of reacting to the rest of the world; that to be happy this time, she must curb the natural human instinct to look up at the sky, with its all-encompassing definition, and gaze towards the immediate ground and horizon, with its lack of shape, or abode, or clear ending.

He was talking about food. He said it would maybe be better if they didn't have an elaborate dinner this time for guests at the reception in the five-star hotel in Calcutta; just some snacks and cocktails.

"You know, things like chicken tikka and kababs," he said. He meant that the meal should be composed of small, disposable items that one could consume and move on, instead of those large repasts that arrested the passage of time and movement. To be left slightly hungry seemed appropriate to the occasion; and when he saw, in his mind's eye, the singed wedges of the tikka, they seemed well suited for this purpose.

Two months later, she and he took separate intercontinental flights to Calcutta. They arrived at the small shed of an international airport with the air of those who'd arrived on a necessary business trip; she was carrying her laptop with her; neither had anything to declare, as they walked, on different afternoons, nonchalantly past the incurious customs officials in the way one might walk down the marriage aisle were all the guests on either side asleep. During the ashirbaad ceremony in her father's flat near Dum Dum, everyone was a degree less solemn than you might have expected them to be; they'd blessed her once before, but they had enough blessings in store to bless her again, with the same untidy shower of grain and grass; there was an element of playacting, as they were not adhering to the plan of the ritual, but imitating what they'd done a few years ago. But there were also unsettling moments of discovery; some of the faces—those of the bridegroom's family—were new, while others were the same. This collision, this bumping into each other, of strangeness and familiarity in the small flat, made the experience something like rereading a well-known story and finding that some of the characters in it had changed while others had remained who they were. Later they all relaxed, like actors after the performance, unmindful of their attire and a slight air of dishevellment. There was a gap of silence, in which Arpita existed

momentarily as if it were her new home. She remembered how
everything had been precisely laid out and premeditated during
the last wedding; how she'd hardly had to move of her own voli-
tion, but had been carried down, as the ceremony pre-ordains,
from her small room in the rented house, down the steps, pre-
cariously, in the arms of her male cousins towards the fire, and
from there to walk blindly behind her husband seven times. She
now saw that house as one she'd never visit again, but which
she'd sleepwalked through, without the aid of her hands and
feet, half afloat, as if she were handicapped but had been somehow given the power to move through its spaces in a supra-
normal way. She said:

"Ranga dadu, it's good to see you looking so well! You're
positively pink!"

"It's the rum that keeps him so healthy," someone else said.
After two weeks, she was looking at the photographs, and she
said: "So many photos! I didn't realise someone was sneaking
around taking so many photos! Who was the photographer?"

"I don't know," he said. Proudly, he added, "I wasn't there."
Naturally, he couldn't be present at his wife-to-be's ashirbaad
ceremony.

They sat looking at the set of photographs. Everyone in
them looked as if they had no desire to go anywhere, and there
was a strange unhurriedness about the faces and postures. It
was almost as if someone had somehow managed to take the
pictures after the event.

Words, silences

TWENTY YEARS HAD PASSED since I last saw him, and when I came out of the room I didn't recognise him at first, though I knew it must be him. Twenty years in books seems like a long time, but linear progression actually has no felt shape; in reality, you always live in the present. Mohon was three times the size he'd been then; and since you don't grow from being medium-sized to huge overnight, he must have had to buy new sets of clothes more than just once.

"Ei Mohon," I said, putting one arm round his shoulder. His bulk pressed against mine, and he smiled. Yet there was an awkwardness between us—where did *that* come from?

"How long are you here for?" I heard myself say. "When are you leaving Calcutta?"

"Hey, day after tomorrow," said Mohon, smiling; and, turning to his wife, he said: "This guy hasn't changed, yaar. He was more or less the same when I saw him last." Romola, in a salwaar kameez, rather pretty, got up from the sofa.

"He's told me so much about you all." At this point the telephone rang shrilly, and I had to raise one palm to indicate I'd be with her directly.

"Hi, I think this must be the first time I'm meeting you," I said, after I'd answered the inconsequential query and put the phone down. Now glasses of soft drink were distributed among us, though I refused mine from the boy who worked in our flat.

"What's it like over there right now?" I meant Tezpur, where he'd been working and living, on an estate, for the last fifteen years. He seemed used to the question, but embarrassed. His wife answered for him.

"It's *boring*!" she said, and then giggled surreptitiously, as if she'd let the cat out of the bag. He answered more seriously, although trying not to sound too serious, "The troubles are always there. You just have to avoid them," making them sound like bacteria you could keep from contracting by observing a careful diet. He said as an afterthought, "Of course you can't always do that."

"Where's your daughter?" I asked suddenly. "Didn't you bring her with you?"

"Ritu," said Mohon, with a deprecating look. "She's gone in with mashi. Mashi came out and took her inside."

"Strange girl! Not in the *least* bit shy," chimed Romola, shaking her head, as if she couldn't believe the person she was speaking of was her daughter. "She just followed your mother inside." And she broodingly took a sip of the pale drink.

So my mother had been out to see them already. She had been present at Mohon's wedding; I'd been away, but of course she'd known Mohon since his birth, because we'd been born around the same time.

Twenty years—I settled back in my chair and said to Mohon:

"But I hear you want to leave that place now? Maybe move to Calcutta?" Mohon leaned forward and nodded his head thoughtfully. All that extra weight had magnified his mottled complexion, which had never been very clear, but there was a strange combination of the effects of aging and an almost untouched simplicity about him. In as polite a way as possible, he said:

"That's right, re. It would be nice." I knew, in fact, that that was why he'd come to Calcutta—not just for a holiday but to see if there might be an "opening," any chance of leaving a landscape made intolerable by strife. But, of course, there was really no great possibility of there being one; opportunities were few.

I looked at him once or twice, and yet we made no eye contact. It was as if all our talk was a prevarication, a hedging about issues. It appeared the unspoken conversations of the last twenty years must now necessarily remain unspoken. He went on to tell me, absently lifting his glass of Fanta, how it would be difficult for him, with the particular background he had, the sort of job he'd been doing for the last ten years, and was now quite comfortable doing, to actually find an opening in Calcutta. The door to my room opened, and Anjali came out with our daughter Priya, whose hair was combed neatly above her forehead, yet untouched in this endangered interval of calm in the day.

Romola straightened a little and smoothed her pale blue salwaar kameez with her fingers.

"She *just* finished her bath," said Anjali (who was wearing a light brown salwaar kameez herself), cheerfully announcing, in medias res, the progress of an episode that concerned us all. "Say hello to Mohon jethu and Romola mashi. Is it jethu or kaku?" she asked, looking at me, distracted. She looked pretty after the bath she herself had had, and the brown salwaar kameez was rather lovely. I looked at her and gave her a smile of recognition you sometimes give someone with whom you spend almost every hour of the day.

"Kaku," said Mohon, ironically but gently; this was the first word he spoke to Anjali. "I narrowly missed being a jethu. He," he tilted his head towards me, "was born just a month before me." Said sardonically but kindly, as if he'd forgiven me for this.

Priya, though, was not at the social hello-saying stage, though she sometimes ingeniously mimicked the sound of that word when she had a telephone in her hands; she just stared and stared at the two of them, as if there was something a little out of the ordinary or embarrassing about them.

"Say something," said Anjali. "Or will will you start talking only when they leave, like you did the other day?" Mohon laughed and shook his head. He was used to the way children are, how perverse and self-willed they can be; his daughter was three years old.

"You know," said Romola, sitting up and looking at Anjali with the intentness of one looking at a photograph, "you look *very* familiar. I'm sure I've seen you before." I looked again at my wife, to see if there might be anything about her face that might be mistaken for someone else's, to see if she reminded me of someone else, and said, "Yes, that's what Romola's been telling me." The two women began to talk about which school they'd been to, but the fact that Romola had been born in Patna and not travelled much out of it seemed to take something of the fire out of the search for where they might have met before.

Left to ourselves, Mohon and I, with our wives' conversation as a background, didn't have a great deal to talk about, but nevertheless kept moving from subject to subject, reminiscing about our childhood as if it were a book we'd both recently read. Among the things mentioned were the pop songs we once liked and were surprised to find we still listened to. "Neil Young, 'Heart of Gold'; that's class stuff, yaar!" Mohon smiled and looked blindly at the wall unit opposite; what rooted him to his armchair, in his over-large half-sleeved shirt and trousers, was not so much weight as some sort of absence, something that had not taken shape and probably never would; possibly the future he'd come looking for in Calcutta. I didn't know how I could help him, though I knew he needed help; the kinds of things we did were so different.

At this point, my mother opened her bedroom door and came out with a girl with lightish hair, almost brownish in colour. She was dressed in a denim jacket and knickerbockers, and could have passed for a Greek or an Italian.

"Oh, *she's* been feeling at home," said Romola, making a can't-help-what-my-daughter-does face.

"Oh, she was very happy, but then just now she began asking for her mother," said my mother. Ritu looked not all there, as if she'd done something wrong; but not overtly repentant. Really, there was nothing to indicate, in the way this family looked, that they'd been living in Tezpur, surrounded by troubles, for the last ten years—Ritu, indeed, had been born there; they could have been from anywhere else, a city suburb.

One thing Mohon remembered from the past was my mother's cooking.

"There never was any comparison! Whenever we used to visit you in Bombay," said Mohon, thinking of the verandah overlooking the sea, "we'd really look forward to mashi's food. Especially the chicken."

"Tell me, re," I said suddenly, asking him what I'd been thinking of asking him for some time, "what about the weight? How did it happen?"

"*This*," he said, as if it were self-evident what "this" was, "happened over the last two or three years, re. I slipped and fell

and fractured my ankle, and the bone's never healed properly."
He smiled and shook his head slightly. "I've had two operations.
But no exercise since then. Otherwise," he turned to Anjali, "I
used to be almost as thin as this guy."

Later, after about twenty minutes, when he said he wanted
to go the toilet, I noticed he walked with a small limp. At one
point I'd ask him, "Where did you fall?" thinking of the hilly
slopes of Assam, but he'd surprise me by saying, "Bombay. When
we went there in 'ninety-seven." When he came back, and we
talked until lunch, we avoided looking at each other, as if there
was something that couldn't be said between us. It was something very minor, elusive, but it wouldn't go away. It could be the
differences that had come about in our respective ways of life,
our different degrees of success, that were now embarrassing
both of us. Or it could be the two small incidents that had occurred those twenty years ago, when we'd spent two nights with
each other, talking, when one thing led to another and culmi-
nated the way such things do, in a mixture of embarrassment
and a cheery, practical resolve to brush it aside. At that time, we
didn't think our actions would have any consequences, and of
course they didn't. What remained was like the smell of smoke,
nothing we could hang on to, but something that wouldn't go
away, no more of an impediment except to keep us from looking
directly at each other. In the end, it had had nothing to do with
our sexuality; it had been one of those nameless animal impulses
common to boys, something between pity and terror; twenty
years later, it left you with nothing to build on, but it was there.

He sat sipping his second Fanta until my mother shouted,
"Lunch!" Mohon and I sat next to each other, my mother and father at the head of the table at opposite ends, and our wives sat
facing us. Ritu and Priya, who'd already been fed, finally began
to play with each other, Ritu, being older, obstreperous, and
over-affectionate, now and then speaking to Priya in, of all

languages, Hindi. Priya tolerated her new friend as long as she didn't touch her too often, until Ritu was frankly puzzled by Priya's changing moods towards her. I could see that Mohon hadn't put on weight only because of his bad foot; he kept taking second and third helpings while protesting he mustn't eat too much.

"It's the same chicken, mashi! Amazing!" he said as we approached the end of the meal, as if the same preparation had been reincarnated today from all those years ago.

All at once Ritu fell asleep, as if she'd inhaled some vapour that causes drowsiness, in an alien house upon a strange bed. Priya, our daughter, kept awake, as she does sometimes late into the night, keeping us awake with her.

"How's your mother, Mohon?" I asked. It had been years since I'd seen her. A small woman with dark eyes and wavy hair, simple, unimposing in her smallness, came back to me. For some reason, he didn't look at me when he said with an odd conviction, "Oh both ma and baba are fine!" They'd both retired, I heard, to their ancestral house in Assam about fifteen years ago; they lived ten miles away from Tezpur. The reason for the return was simple: Mohon had got into "bad company" in his college in Delhi, into drugs, and the only route that lay before them was to remove him entirely from the influence of his friends, from the busyness of the metropolis, to the ancestral home in Assam. They'd seemed to doubt that he'd otherwise have the power to resist the influence on his own.

"Tell him to lose weight," I said to Romola, leaning forward. "At this age it might seem okay, but his . . ." I gestured around the region of his heart.

"You tell him," she whispered. Twenty years! The afternoon moved towards teatime with its shingaras, after which they would leave. All those changes; Assam, Calcutta; and yet we seemed happy in our marriages, with our small families. Our wives were very different from each other, perhaps even from us, but our lives had come to occupy fully the shapes they'd made for them. Whatever had happened between us all those years ago had become harmless, meaningless, at most an uncomfortable scab that, with the friction of history, would fall off at some time. Was that the fate of these small excitements, that they became mawkish and disownable in the future?

Yet I hoped that his purpose was served. If there was going to be an opening, I'm sure my father would remember Mohon, and that he was ready to be transferred to Calcutta. I forgot to obey Romola's instructions, and didn't say anything to Mohon except "Try to cut down on the beer." He looked at me, the old look of friendship, and sighed, "Yeah, that's the one thing I must do."

When he got up to go, heavy, his figure bigger than I could remember, I looked at his limp and expected it to disappear any minute, because it seemed to come from a callus under his foot that was destined to fade.

The Party

THE DINNER HAD BEEN appointed for, first, Friday, then Saturday night, and already, by the middle of the week, the preparations had begun. They—the small nuclear family of father, mother, and the son who was equal to an army of a hundred—were going to move from this rather equanimous accommodation to a larger flat in another locality in a couple of weeks, so this would probably be the last party Mrs. Sinha-Roy would be hosting in some time. Not that the flat was a small one; in fact, it had spaces they didn't know what do with. But with Mr. Sinha-Roy's ascension to head of finance a few months ago, there was the technicality that the flat had only two bedrooms, just a technicality, since the bedrooms were huge, but yet a two-bedroom flat was not quite commensurate with the position of a head of finance and, more practically, his "entertainment" requirements. From now on, he would be expected to throw larger parties.

The young son, Amal, no more than eight years old, lorded it over the servants—the cook, the bearer, the maidservant—as the preparations made progress, now entering the disorderly activity of the kitchen, now rushing past or circling the sari-clad, abstracted figure of Mrs. Sinha-Roy as if she were some kind of portal. There was an enigmatic aura about him that couldn't be quite pinpointed; as if he weren't just the head of finance's son, but as if there resided in him, in some indirect but undeniable way, the hopes and aspirations of the company Mr. Sinha-Roy worked for; as if he were in some way its secret and unacknowledged symbol. It wasn't enough that the franchise of happiness the company offered lay in the furniture and the flat and the other "perquisites"; and that Mr. Sinha-Roy would, as head of finance, have to negotiate large losses and gains. The boy, too, was part of that loss and gain in a way he didn't quite understand.

"What time's Sinha-Roy's dinner?" asked Mr. Gupta, glassy-eyed, scratching his stubble as he cruised that morning down Marine Drive. In the office, he referred to Sinha-Roy as "sir" or "Mr. Sinha-Roy," but in private he derived a careless, imperious pleasure from dropping the awed monosyllabic whisper of the first word or the ingratiating, lisping two syllables of the "Mr." This was one of the small freedoms of "company life": that, however it may have ingrained itself into you as a religion, you did not have to practise it at home. Driving down Marine Drive, Mr. Gupta was a free man; though only in a sense, because the car on whose steering wheel his hands rested was an accessory of the company's, both a free-moving object that gave him the illusion of ownership and control, and an accomplice to employment.

"Seven-thirty," said Mrs. Arati Gupta, brushing aside the filigree of hair that had blown across her face with the breeze. She was the less sharp but the more pragmatic, even the wiser, of the two. In a sense, she was the one behind the wheel, always had been, always would be, while he made the protestations and clamour of the engine. "But eight o'clock would be all right, don't you think?" always seeking his agreement, if not permission, at the end of a suggestion.

The palm trees of Marine Drive rushed in the opposite direction, like a crowd that was running to meet someone. Only recently, Mrs. Gandhi had waved a wand—or was it a cane?—and nationalised all the banks, and substantially reduced foreign shareholdings in "private sector" companies. This was true of the private sector company, which manufactured paint, where Mr. Gupta worked, which recently had been made more "Indian" or true-blooded but whose status derived from the fact that it had once, not long ago, had the word "British" in its name (the word had now, with dignity, been dispensed with). The private sector found itself uneasily on the cusp of a world that had been left behind and which Mrs. Gandhi, reportedly, had set about changing.

"Yes, eight o'clock; I don't want to go too early," he said, taking a bend. Mrs. Gupta said, as if the thought had just come to her: "Should we take something for them?" There were, of course, no rules on this matter, of visiting your superior's house on what was after all a social and civilised visit, no rules except when you realised that every form of interaction was permeated by company law, not the sort of company law that Mr. Gupta had studied laboriously what seemed not many years ago, but the kind that Arati Gupta had become an avid student of.

"I don't know," said her husband gruffly. "It's not done. People will talk." "People"; "them": simple, collective pronouns and nouns that had, however, complex but exclusive gradations in the life they'd made their own. "People" was not only managers, heads of sections, and directors, but their wives, too. "Them" had the ability to take on different, often contesting, resonances: right now it conveyed, at once, both Mr. and Mrs. Sinha-Roy and the difference between them as individuals.

"What about the son, what about Amal," said Mrs. Gupta tranquilly. "We should take him a little something."

It was as if she were testing him; she liked teasing him at times.

"What about Amal!" he said, mimicking her. "He doesn't need anything. Don't be silly!" His face had a special vehemence of emotion that came into being when he knew he'd be called upon to display a fatherliness that he did not possess. Somehow, the boy—the idea of him, not even the boy himself—exhausted him more than anything else.

In the Sinha-Roys' flat, the cook, a dark septuagenarian, woke up from a brief nap to finish frying the little patties he'd set aside for the afternoon. The driver rang the bell and came in holding a bouquet of flowers; and Mrs. Sinha-Roy, like a somnambulist in her housecoat, moved from dining table to living room and back again in the heat of the afternoon, distributing flowers from one vase to another.

The whole day seemed like an eternity to the boy, especially when holiday and party happened to coincide in a chance intermission. He had no homework he needed to attack immediately; instead he had this sense of a function, a role that had come to him out of nowhere, a calling that he was equal to.

By evening the guests and colleagues, before they left their houses, had begun to apply the finishing touches—aftershave lotion on the cheeks, the last fold of the sari smoothed till it seemed exactly in place. And, at home, like some unappeasable master of ceremonies, Amal tasted the savouries, which were either brought to him on a plate with a glass of cola, or which he himself chose at random.

The Guptas were, as it happened, the first to arrive; they

must look suitably grateful, because they were to occupy this flat from the twenty-third of the month; they needed to put in an appearance before anyone else. On the way, Mrs. Gupta had bought herself a fragrant mogra from a girl and put it in her hair. The flat itself was on display; every preparatory movement had stopped, and the drawing room had a finished look about it, as if a work of art had reached its public, final version.

Gradually, the other guests began to trickle in, the doorbell was rung, and each couple greeted with varying degrees of surprise, recognition, and familial warmth. "Where's Amal?" everyone wanted to know, as if the solution to this party lay not in its social hierarchies, or in the longer-term destinies it vaguely pointed to, but in where, and who, the boy was. Because the party, after all, was a serious business.

As the party moved on, and the evening darkened outside with the intermittent light of other buildings, Atul Gupta found himself, at nine o'clock, alone and moorless for a few minutes in the corridor, with a drink in his hand. He realised, with a sort of tentativeness that was rarely visible but had been reserved for his first days in the office, which had been naked then but was apparelled in decent clothes since, that the door not far away from him, which had been left slightly ajar and from which a bright light was shining, was the boy's door. He saw his ambition and fear and curiosity had preceded him here and were waiting like a shadow outside it. He cleared his throat and, taking a few steps forward, knocked.

"Come in," said a small voice from within. Mr. Gupta's heart beat a little faster. He pushed the door by the handle; the beast, or god, or mystery, the company's inmost secret, however you chose to view him, was sitting there at the edge of his bed, a glass of cola on the floor before him, a drawing book in his hand. This was the head of finance's innermost sanctum, this was where his life and heart beat, and he, Assistant Company Secretary, must, against his own wishes, surrender and bow his head silently before it. On a bright red carpet lay, innocently, three or four dinky toys, including an overturned truck; stopping near it as if it might go off if he touched it, Mr. Gupta said:

"How are you, young man?" The boy turned to look at him; and Mr. Gupta flinched, as if his future, or what little he knew of it, had turned to look at him in that air-conditioned room and judged him; for these were not his boss's eyes, but the eyes that, invisibly, ruled and governed his boss's life. He had not known, before he'd begun, that company life concealed such mysteries; the Managing Director's children were long grown up and lived abroad, in England. It was here, then, that, by default, all that was sweet and virginal and innocent about the company dwelt, a savage whose mind was far removed from adult reasoning and the laws that governed adult life.

"Hello, Uncle Atul," said the boy, without much interest. "I'm fine, thank you."

"May I sit down?" said Mr. Gupta, smiling, but feeling as if he were straining against a hidden door that wouldn't open.

"Yes, Uncle," said Amal, glumly preparing for a conversation. The man sat at the edge of the bed, as if he'd been told to by a wave of the hand. The company itself had never been so perfunctory with him.

"Nice room you have," he said, uttering a truth in a hapless way to make it sound like a lie. When, in the past, he'd presented his reports and the relevant taxation figures to his superiors, even the worst-compiled of them had more conviction than his platitude. The question that short-sighted politicians and bureaucrats had been asking of companies such as his—was it worth it?—the toothpaste, the colas, the enamel paint, the butter—was one he suddenly found asking himself. He picked up a dinky toy and put it down again.

The boy said nothing; then, moving his body towards Mr.

Gupta, handed him the large drawing book he had in his hands.

"I drew these pictures today," he said quietly, without modesty but without bravado, either.

"Oh, that's nice!" said Mr. Gupta, finding it easier to lie as time wore on, staring at the clumsy figures in blue and yellow as if they were some sort of cipher, or somehow part of that other, more recalcitrant code he was trying to interpret. He bent his head, almost submissively, and said, "What's this?"

He looked very gravely at a misshapen green creature, obviously an animal in the early days of its evolution, with what looked like rain falling behind it. It was as if the creature had floated out of nowhere into his immediate vision.

"That's a horse," said the boy, simply. "That's the sky," pointing to the crowded blue strokes. The man nodded slowly like one who, without realising it, had been made more knowledgeable, as indeed he had; what had seemed like clouds in his confused, self-created landscape, massed and obfuscating, were resolving themselves into ordinary shapes and forms.

Not finished, he noted a scarecrow-like figure with large eyes. Cheerfully, as if he were now more adept at this game, he asked:

"What's this?" The boy picked up the tepid cola from the floor and sipped it as the man respectfully waited for an answer.

"That's baba," the boy revealed casually. Mr. Gupta started; he felt a secret had been revealed to him that no one else in the company knew. So this was how his father, Gupta's own boss, appeared in the eyes of what was hidden, what lay at the source of questions and solutions that he would not be able to understand. Quickly he asked, still struggling to put his impulses into words:

"Any pictures of you? Or Ma? Or your friends—your best friend?" The boy closed the drawing book restlessly; Mr. Gupta feared his interview was going to be cut short. The sound of the air conditioner grew in its confidential presence. But he must continue; having been drawn in, he now felt excluded, as if a promise of something, something concrete, had been suggested to him, and immediately withdrawn. Where was he to go now? And if he did not go on, it would not be the boy, or the company, but himself he would be left to blame. In the end, you became your own accuser.

Not the boy, but a warm breath of air from the corridor interrupted him, as the door opened farther and Mrs. Sinha-Roy said cheerfully:

"Amal, where have you been? Mrs. Mehra wants to see you, and there are others waiting for you outside." Mr. Gupta turned to see Mrs. Sinha-Roy, resplendent in her pink Parsi sari, at the door, and Mrs. Mehra, large and solid and smiling behind her, one of the overhead lights shining in her eyes. He knew then that all his years of hard work and preparation and dissembling and dreaming would get him no further than where he was.

"I was talking to Uncle Atul," said the boy, as if this self-evident fact needed his witness to bring it to conclusion.

Confession of a sacrifice

I AM BEING PREPARED for a sacrifice. This honour has bowed my head, above all the honours that people might give me. I walk in fear and humility, not quite following the significance of my function.

People are not only nice to me; they are tender with me. They are waiting for the big day to arrive. They have started constructing their shrines, making their preparations. Whenever I walk into the club, people stop eating and give me a second look; it's as if they realize their food's a shadow in comparison to the sanctity of my blood, my meat.

The other day I was sitting in the club with an old friend, someone close to my father's age who has known me for years. He was in the navy blue suit he always prefers to wear, and there were chop suey and two bowls of clear soup before us. We were bent, absorbed, over our bowls of soup, and my friend, Mr. Dastur, asked me how my little one was doing.

"Oh, he's fine," I said. "He's been going to school for a year now." Mr. Dastur has never really been interested in small talk, although we make nothing but small talk, and he called out distractedly to a waiter to bring him some chili sauce.

"My grandson's in the fifth standard," he said. "He's turning out to be a real smart chhokra." Suddenly a look came to his eyes, not the kind of look he'd had when he was calling for the waiter, but an untranslatable look, something I'd rarely seen in his eyes, something that went to the very depths of his being.

"You know," he said, looking at his soup, "you've surprised us all. I never thought, when you were a child, that . . ." I shook my head, not knowing what to say. There are some things human beings are still not articulate about; not even I, although my profession's connected with words.

At first, I didn't quite know. I didn't know why people were nice to me, why they came and shook my hand and wanted to listen to my every word. I was interviewed by various newspapers; sometimes I'd be woken out of sleep by the sound of the phone ringing, not knowing, in my semi-awake startlement, what it all meant, as if my mind were still reluctant to emerge from the dream it was having, or had begun, without effort, to confuse dream and reality. In my daytime world, I was invited everywhere; everyone recognised me as soon as I walked in, and their voices took on a different kind of tone, their faces hovered between awe and inscrutability. Consuls and ambassadors invited me to their houses; they fed me the best food; when I went to a new city, I was kept in the most elegant hotels. Gradually, one day, or in the course of a number of days, it dawned on me—I don't remember who told me—that I was being prepared for the sacrifice, that I'd become involved with something much bigger than I could understand, that my life had become, in some way, connected to the nebulous common good and its continuing life.

I am truly privileged. Over the centuries known to man, right from time's consciousness, from the dawning of light on rudimentary societies, there were a few who were chosen. They didn't lead the life that "normal" people do; they were set apart from others, pampered, worshipped. Their long preparation was always a mystery. Their clan's, or tribe's, dreams and hopes—something more than dreams and hopes, something I still find difficult to express—became theirs; their passing and return were celebrated in shrines, as they are now in newspapers. So it was then; so it is now.

I have begun my preparation. I had begun it even when I was not, could not be, altogether conscious of doing so, and continue it even when I believe I am immersed in other things. Long before the actual day arrives, you begin the sacrifice, you hand over your life, you allow bits and pieces of yourself to be taken from you. At the same time, you are loved, not for what you are (and what are you, anyway, what were you before all this began?) but for what you can give, and the immense gift you will bestow on everyone in the future. That day has not yet come. In the meanwhile, in the last, extraordinary days of my preparation, I accept, with good grace and humility, the curiosity and reverence that others direct towards me. There are a few who spit on me, because they think I am not worthy.

The Old Masters

HE GLANCED at his watch and made an attempt to finish the tea in his cup; he was waiting for a call, and it was his second cup of tea. Five minutes later, the phone began to ring.

"Pramathesh?" said the voice at the other end; and he could tell, from its slight note of insouciance and boredom, that it was Ranjit.

"I was waiting for your call, old man," he said, trying to muffle his irritation with his usual show of joviality. "You were supposed to call half an hour ago." He didn't know why he even bothered to mention this, since Ranjit, who was never known to acknowledge he was late, would take this to be an unnecessarily pedantic remark, a remark that pointed to the actual, if generally concealed, gulf that distinguished their temperaments.

"Trying to send the boy off to school . . . didn't want to go this morning," Ranjit muttered. "That boy'll cost me my job one of these days."

"Come, come, don't blame it on poor Mithu. He has enough troubles being an innocent bystander in your life. Are we ready?"

"Of course I'm ready! Should we say ten minutes?" As an afterthought, a change of register: "Sorry I didn't call earlier." You can't choose your colleagues in the office; he hadn't grasped the significance of this until a few months ago. And to pretend you were friends—that, too, was a fiction you couldn't bring yourself to wholly believe in, but couldn't entirely dispense with either; you did "things" together, sometimes outside office hours, you visited each other's houses—he'd been to Ranjit's place in New Alipore only day before yesterday—got to know each other's wives and children, the kind of food the wife, affectionately referred to as the "grihini," cooked, and, yet, you made a pact to keep all that was true and most important about yourself from the colleague; in case the desirable boundary between private life and secret nightmare and employment ceased to exist. Meanwhile, your *real* friends, those mythological beings, who by now had embarked on lives and careers of their own, fell obligingly by the wayside; they became things you put inside a closet and meant to recover, someday, in the future. In other words, you were alone, with your family, and your destiny.

Pramathesh Majumdar had joined the company three years ago, soon after coming back from England in 1964 as a chartered accountant. A brief honeymoon period with office life and work in Calcutta ensued, which also saw this makeshift arrangement, this friendship, with Ranjit Biswas come into being. Ranjit had never been abroad; he'd been born and brought up in Calcutta. He had the ease and the unquestioning expectancy of routine repeating itself, and of things continuing to fit, that belong to one who has never been removed from his original habitat. Pramathesh belonged nowhere; he came, originally, from East Bengal; his sights were probably set somewhere higher. Although Ranjit Biswas was still, strictly speaking, a colleague, both knew, though this wasn't articulated, that Pramathesh, in his unassuming way, was preparing himself for the race people called "professional life," while Ranjit, with his impatience at keeping appointments, was perhaps going to stay in the same place for some time, feeling, now and then, bitter, without being unduly bothered to do anything about it. It was the strength of Pramathesh's British degree that gave him a head start, of course, but it was also something else, a meticulousness that might be called foresight. In fact, Pramathesh had been transferred to the Delhi office in June this year, and since the Delhi office was now the head office, this move had been interpreted as a promotion.

Today's mission was the outcome of a chance remark made day before yesterday. He'd been sitting at Ranjit's place after dinner, contemplating returning to the guest house; he said, stretching his arms, "Well, I'm returning to Delhi next week. Have to get down to some shopping." "Like what, Pramathesh da?" asked Ranjit's wife, Malini, as she was putting away the dishes. "The usual things, I suppose," said Pramathesh, who looked younger than his thirty-nine years. "Go to Gariahat, buy a few saris; decorations; take some gandharaj lime—my son loves those . . ." In his heart of hearts, he missed Calcutta; Delhi seemed small and transitory and provincial in comparison. "How did the project with the boss go this time?" asked Ranjit, lighting a cigarette (his wife called him a "chain-smoker") and leaning against the wicker chair in the verandah. There was curiosity in his voice, and a hint of competitiveness. "Oh, all right," said Pramathesh, sounding noncommittal, but actually engrossed in the mental picture of Lahiri as it hovered before him, a quiet, balding man with fair, tissue-paper-like skin who wore glasses with thick lenses and looked as if nothing had changed noticeably since the years before Independence. He could hear his voice and his cough. "You know, generous and friendly when he's in a good mood, and slightly unfathomable when he's not." Ranjit nodded and took a fresh puff on his cigarette. "Are you thinking of taking back a two-kilogram rui from the fish market?" said Malini from the semi-lit dining room, her voice holding back laughter. "I saw you eating today and thought, 'He doesn't get fish there.'" "Yes, that's right," said Pramathesh, "I'll just give it to the air hostess and tell her to hang on to it until we land." "A lot of people take back mishti doi," said Ranjit. He began to laugh in his unobtrusively nasty, dry manner, which meant that he was going to reveal something that had given him pleasure at someone else's expense. "I saw a man standing in line for security at the airport with a huge bhaad of doi, and the next time I saw him the bhaad had fallen to ground and shattered, the yoghurt lay on the floor in a tragic mess: the poor man, he looked lost and heartbroken! I don't think we'll see him in Calcutta in a hurry!" After a few moments, Pramathesh said quietly, "I was thinking of taking back a picture . . . something nice—to hang up in the new flat." "A picture?"

There were still hardly any art galleries in Calcutta. And the idea of buying a painting—and not a print—was still an unusual one. But recently, at a cocktail party in a superior's bungalow in Delhi, Pramathesh's wife had noticed an original Nandalal Bose. Not that she'd known it was an original; but someone told her it was. Returning to their flat, she'd said it might be a good idea to buy a decent painting for their drawing room; it would be their first stab at creating a status that would be in accordance with Pramathesh's professional life. Now, Ranjit racked his brains and said, "Well, I know where Gopal Ghosh lives; we could go there." Of course, owning a Gopal Ghosh may not be owning a Picasso; but his paintings were held in high regard. Just as Pramathesh's career as a chartered accountant and an employee was at the fledgling stage, so was the Indian art world, with its ambivalences and lack of self-belief. Paradoxically, it was those who might be accused of not understanding art who would nourish it, unknowingly, through this delicate moment, setting up a concomitance between its life and theirs. It was as if their lives were destined, in some sense, to be connected and to grow together, though this must not be seen to be so.

So the two men decided to meet in front of the office itself in Chowringhee, at a quarter past ten on Saturday, before the seven-storeyed building. An old, moustached watchman who had nothing much to occupy him hovered in the background while Pramathesh waited for Ranjit to arrive. When he did, Pramathesh instructed his driver to remain parked where he was. From there, they went in Ranjit's white Ambassador, the driver in front wordless, down a main artery, which was fairly deserted on a Saturday, towards one of the by-lanes in an area quite far from both New Alipore and the company guest house; Pramathesh, in fact, didn't know what it was called. Here, they came to a ground-floor flat in an old two-storeyed house in a narrow lane facing, and flanked by, other houses not unlike itself. They were not sure if they should just walk in, but when they did, finding the door open, they saw no one inside; only the ceiling fan hung immobile above them. The painter, emerging into the living room a few minutes later to discover them, didn't seem to mind their intrusion. He was wearing a dhoti and a shabby jacket himself, and looked abstracted; he glanced at the two men in their pressed shirtsleeves, trousers, and sandals, and appeared to make a shrewd appraisal of why they were here and who they might be. "Was it you who just came up in the car?" he asked, to which Pramathesh said, a little hesitantly, "Yes." He finally sold Pramathesh two of his paintings very matter-of-factly, bringing them from a room inside, one showing a pale, white forest, in which the trees were crested with white blossoms, with probably a peasant woman walking in it, and the other of a group of figures, possibly pilgrims, walking dimly past a mountainside. One might have missed their appeal; indeed, Pramathesh had to summon up something forgotten inside him, something from his early youth, in order to respond to them. It was not a faculty he had to use often, or of late; and he wasn't altogether sure of his judgement. At any rate, without quite knowing why, he bought the two paintings for one hundred and fifty rupees each.

Two days later, Pramathesh left Calcutta. As had been apparent, he continued, as the next decade unfolded, to do substantially better than Ranjit Biswas. His rise surprised even him. Ranjit remained more or less stationary, with the prospect of a small promotion in the next five years; while Pramathesh was transferred to Bombay, and made general manager at the Bombay branch. The last old master he bought was a Jamini Roy, in 1969, again on a visit to Calcutta in the winter. By then, Calcutta was in decline; the branch was experiencing a series of lockouts, and Ranjit was sounding more and more beleaguered and nonplussed, as if he'd just found out that he was fighting the battle alone. "It's difficult to be in control anymore, bhai. They"—he meant the workers—"are the bosses now; we run behind them," he said, a little self-conscious in his defensiveness, and partly because Pramathesh was now, technically, no longer a colleague; the old banter had a slight fakeness about it. Jamini Roy was already an old man, and, during this visit, Pramathesh went to the painter's house with Amita, his wife, small and bright in a printed silk sari, about to assume life in Bombay; the old man, in a vest and dhoti, tottered out, and signed the paintings on the floor. When asked innocently by Amita, "What time of the day do you paint?" he responded like any cantankerous old man, "How can I answer that? Can I tell you when I eat, or drink, or sleep?" Upside down on the floor before them lay the paintings, the ideal figures with over-large eyes that did not see, the repetitive shapes in repose.

It's not as if Pramathesh and Amita Majumdar spent too much time thinking about these paintings; Bombay didn't give one much time to think. They moved from drawing room to drawing room as the couple themselves moved about in Bombay, from Worli to Kemp's Corner to Malabar Hill. And it wasn't as if they were insensitive to art; nor were they pretentiously artistic; they were content to display them, respectfully, on the walls. Of course, they—the paintings—did coincide with that part of the couple that was defined by their natural ambition, by Pramathesh's career and his concern for the future, but in an odd way, so that the paintings somewhat transcended, or ignored, these vivid concerns. They were probably an unexplored part of their lives. Meanwhile, Jamini Roy, who'd already seemed so old, died peacefully in 1972. Gopal Ghosh died in penury and neglect about five years later, his last days an alcoholic stupor, often drinking himself to sleep on the pavement, and being carried home by passersby.

On subsequent visits to Calcutta (and they did need to make visits, because they had relatives here, and occasionally there were weddings), Pramathesh and his wife were spared the embarrassment of having to meet the Biswases too frequently, because Ranjit had lost his job and joined a Marwari company that made ceiling and table fans, where he seemed reasonably happy, and able to conceal from himself the fact that here, too, the prospects for advancement were of a limited nature. But he had a better position than before; and, since Pramathesh was appointed to the Board in 1977, it was just as well they didn't meet except in the lobby of the Calcutta Club by accident, or at Lake Market, where they came upon each other with surprised exclamations and hurriedly exchanged pleasantries before saying goodbye. Former colleagues are happy to meet and depart from each other like ghosts, in an evanescent zone of their own making that lies somewhere between their working life, leisure time, memory, and the future. Nothing is final about these meetings until they retire, and they can review the shape of their achievements. Even then, their children, who may have entirely forgotten one another, have the potential to carry on their fathers' rivalries and friendships without knowing it, in their parents' drifting, speculative daydreams. Anyway, Ranjit leaving his job and disappearing in another direction saved Pramathesh the minor embarrassment of having to be his superior, and preside over his career.

The main surprise in Pramathesh's life came from his son, who took up the violin and Western classical music in a serious way when he was a teenager. What had begun as an eccentric but admirable pursuit after school hours became something more than that. One day, the boy came back from school and said, "Baba, I want to study the violin." Pramathesh was too disarmed to raise an objection just then; and, as he remained unable to come up with one after two, then three, years, he saw, fondly but with a lurking feeling of helplessness, that his son would level out what he had striven for, that all the sense of certainty and dull, precious predictability and self-sufficiency he had naively built up would now—he was almost grateful for it— become, whether his son succeeded or not (because success in the arts counts for so little), less quantifiable, like a new beginning. His son and grandchildren would lead a life quite different from what he'd thought they would. He sent his son to study the violin in London, and this rendered him almost bankrupt, though his "almost bankrupt" was still substantially better off than most of his countrymen. He and Amita moved, after his retirement in the mid-eighties, to a spacious apartment in West Bandra which he had bought twelve years ago for two lakh rupees; they lived here alone, with a servant, going out together now and then to walk in the lane, while their son, finally, settled in the U.S. and married there, making several abortive attempts to inaugurate a career as a musician. The paintings went with them to Bandra, and gazed upon Pramathesh's life without understanding its trajectory, but forgiving it nevertheless by not giving it too much importance. Now and then he gazed back at the paintings, considering what, or who, had given birth to that procession of figures by the mountainside, or that pale forest; those shadowy colours pointed to something he was still content, in his deliberate withdrawal from the imagination, not to understand. Jamini Roy, however, stayed in the drawing room, immutable; and Gopal Ghosh, who had been forgotten by the art world and then lately recovered and re-estimated, was like an enigma that had glancingly touched Pramathesh's working and his private life, near and utterly distant. The world that had produced that curious art, those daubs of green and bold lines, that one never knew, in the end, what to think of, had long ceased to exist; he had made an inroad towards it, by chance, for some other reason, and touched it without ever entering it anything but superficially. History, as if to compensate for that passing, and in a belated consciousness of its own importance, had added to the paintings a value that neither Pramathesh nor the painters would have at first dreamt of; while taking away from him, gradually, his working life, his youth, and the bustling innocence of his adult certainties.

An Infatuation

(From the *Ramayana*)

SHE'D BEEN WATCHING the two men for a while, and the pale, rather docile, wife with vermilion in her hair, who sometimes went inside the small house and came out again. She'd been watching from behind a bush, so they hadn't seen her; they had the air of being not quite travellers, nor people who'd been settled for long; but they looked too composed to be fugitives. Sometimes the men went away into the forest while the woman attended to household chores—Surpanakha observed this interestedly from a distance—and then they'd return with something she'd chop and cook, releasing an aroma that hung incongruously around the small house.

She, when she considered herself, thought how much stronger and more capable she would be than that radiantly beautiful but more or less useless woman, how she'd not allow the men to work at all, and do everything for them herself. It was the taller one she'd come to prefer; the older one, whose every action had such authority. She liked to watch him bending, or brushing away a bit of dust from his dhoti, or straightening swiftly, with that mixture of adroitness and awkwardness that only human beings, however godly they are, have; he was so much more beautiful than she was. It was not his wife's beauty she feared and envied; it was his. Sighing, she looked at her own muscular arms, used to lifting heavy things and throwing them into the distance, somewhat hirsute and dark but undoubtedly efficient, and compared them to his, which glowed in the sunlight. Her face, which she'd begun to look at in a pond nearby, had cavernous nostrils and tiny tusks that jutted out from beneath her lips; it was full of fierceness and candour, but, when she cried, it did not evoke pity, not even her own. The face reflected on the water filled her with displeasure. How lovely his features were in comparison!

After about six days had passed, and she'd gone unnoticed, hiding, frightened, and when she was glimpsed, frightening, behind the bush, she decided to approach him. She had grown tired of hovering there like an animal; even the animals had begun to watch her. Although she'd been taught to believe, since childhood, that rakkhoshes were better—braver, less selfish, more charitable, and better-natured—than human beings and gods, it was true the latter were prettier. They'd been blessed unfairly by creation; no one knew why. Long ago she'd been told that it was bad luck to fall in love with a god or a human being, but the possibility had seemed so remote that she'd never entertained it seriously. The feeling of longing, too, was relatively new for her, although she was in full maturity as a woman; but she was untried and untested, rakkhosh though she was, and uncourted; and this odd condition of restlessness was more solitary and inward, she found, than indigestion, and more painful.

She decided to change herself. She could take other forms at will, albeit temporarily; she decided to become someone else, at least for a while. She went to a clearing where she was sure no one would see her, where the only living things were some insects and a few birds on the trees, and the transformation took place. Now she went to the pond to look at the picture in the water. Her heart, like a girl's upon glimpsing a bride, beat faster at what she saw; a woman with large eyes and long hair coming down to her waist, her body pliant. She wasn't sure if this was her, or if the water was reflecting someone else.

Ram and his younger brother Lakshman had gone out into the forest to collect some wood; she saw them from a distance. Her mouth went dry, and she snorted with nervousness; then she recalled how she'd become more beautiful than she'd imagined, and tried to control these noises she inadvertently made. She thought, looking at Ram, "He is not a man; I'm sure he's a god," and was filled with longing. When they came nearer her, she lost her shyness and came out into the clearing.

"What's this?" said Ram softly to his brother, pretending not to have seen her. Lakshman glanced back quickly and whispered, as he bent to pick up his axe:

"I don't know—but this beautiful 'maiden' smells of rakkhoshi; look at the gawky and clumsy way she carries her body, as if it were an ornament she'd recently acquired."

"Let's have some fun with her," whispered Ram. He'd been bored for days in the forest, and this overbearing, obstreperous creature of ethereal beauty, now approaching them with unusually heavy footsteps, promised entertainment.

"Lord . . . ," she stuttered, ". . . Lord . . . forgive me for intruding so shamelessly, but I saw you wandering alone and thought you might have lost your way." Ram and Lakshman looked at each other; their faces were grave, but a smile glinted in their eyes. They'd noticed she'd ignored Lakshman altogether.

It amused and flattered Ram to be on the receiving end of this attention, even if it came from a rakkhoshi who'd changed shape; and it also repelled him vaguely. He experienced, for the first time, the dubious and uncomfortable pleasure of being the object of pursuit. This didn't bother him unduly, though; he was, like all members of the male sex, slightly vain. Lakshman cleared his throat and said:

"Who are you, maiden? Do you come from these parts?"

"Not far from here," said the beautiful woman, while the covering on her bosom slipped a little without her noticing it. "Lord," she said, going up to Ram and touching his arm, "let's go a little way from here. There's a place not far away where you can get some rest." Within the beautiful body, the rakkhoshi's heart beat fiercely, but with trepidation.

"I don't mind," said the godly one slowly. "But what's a woman like you doing here alone? Aren't you afraid of thieves?"

"I know no fear, Lord," she said. "Besides, seeing you, whatever fear I might have had melts away."

"Before I go with you," conceded Ram, "I must consult my brother—and tell him what to do when I've gone." Surpanakha said: "Whatever pleases you, Lord," but thought, "I've won him over; I can't believe it. My prayers are answered."

Ram went to Lakshman and said: "This creature's beginning to tire me. Do something."

"Like what?" said Lakshman. He was sharpening the blade of his knife. Ram admired the back of his hand and said moodily:

"I don't know. Something she'll remember for days. Teach her a lesson for being so forward." Lakshman got up wearily with the knife still in one hand, and Ram said under his breath:

"Don't kill her, though."

A little later, a howl was heard. Lakshman came back; there was some blood on the blade. "I cut her nose," he said. "It"—he gestured towards the knife—"went through her nostril as if it were silk. She immediately changed back into the horrible creature she really is. She's not worth describing," he said, as he wiped his blade and Ram chuckled without smiling. "She was in some pain. She flapped her arms and screamed in pain and ran off into the forest like some agitated beast."

Crying and screaming, Surpanakha circled around the shrubs and trees, dripping blood. The blood was mingled with the snot that came from her weeping, and she wiped these away from her disfigured face without thinking. Even when the pain had subsided a little, the bewilderment remained, that the one she'd worshipped should be so without compassion, so unlike what he looked like. It was from here, in this state, she went looking for Ravan.

The Wedding

SEVERAL MILLENNIA HAD PASSED, and Shiv was still meditating, now and then coming out of his trance to take a few long-drawn-out puffs of ganja, then returning, his eyes red, to the trance again. The tiger skin on his shoulder was dark and hung loosely. From the knots of his hair, which looked as if it hadn't been washed for centuries, the Ganga poured out, a trickle. The crescent moon, like a cheap trinket you might buy at Kalighat, was also lodged in the matted hair. The forehead was covered with ash that hadn't been wiped away in a long time; the only thing faintly resplendent was the third eye, which, whenever it opened, shone with more light than the moon.

Meanwhile, worlds ended, began; and the sun rose and set behind him, making the peaks of Kailash dazzle whitely and mutely during the day, casting a pale orange glow upon them at the time of its disappearance. Night came; and then it ebbed away after a few hours, and the sun rose again, slowly.

Vishnu muttered to a friend:

"Well, it's time he woke up."

The friend shuddered.

"There's such a to-do when he does."

Vishnu said:

"I wish our gods had, now and again, bouts of insomnia, and that their samadhis were a little less deep. Waking them means so much expenditure, that the three worlds are impoverished for years to come, and no living creature, with all the noise, can sleep for days . . ." He sighed, didn't quite seem to be himself; then called out: "Kama!"

The god, suspended in air, about to release an arrow from his bow, heard the call. Distracted, abandoning his task, and leaving the couple below silent, he appeared before the Preserver of the Universe.

"You called, Lord," he said. Vishnu nodded. He said something in his ear; Kama paled.

"N-not that," he stammered. "I'd be undone!" Vishnu waved a hand casually. "You might be temporarily put out of action, no more," he said calmingly. "Besides, you can't die—remember? We need him; he has duties to attend to. All he does is meditate, play his damru a little, and smoke ganja with his cohorts. He's become most unsociable in the ordinary sense of the word."

"I've always kept my distance from him," said Kama fastidiously.

"So have I," said Vishnu. "Anyway, think about it . . ."

"Have I a choice?" asked Kama, already thinking of how to extricate himself. Vishnu read his mind.

"I'm afraid not . . . ," he said somewhat lugubriously.

THE DAUGHTER OF the Himalayas had thought of going out that day with two friends, of walking about and exploring the surrounding scenery. She was sixteen years old; less mature, in a sense, than other girls her age; impulsive, moody, and tending to depend too much on other people's advice. She spent large tracts of time doing what she considered nothing; for instance, yesterday she'd had a music lesson that had lasted for hours; at other times, she daydreamed, which to her was more fruitful activity. She was preparing—but for what? No exam, certainly. She had two friends, Nandini and Rajeshwari, in whom she confided, but with whom she also quarrelled. And the workings of the palace went on about her (she was hardly mindful of them) with an immense, tiresome regularity.

Up she went the slopes now, followed by her friends.

"Parvati, wait!" said Nandini, panting. The three friends loitered occasionally beneath a tree to gossip, sometimes for as long as half an hour. When they felt hungry, they regretted that they hadn't brought any food with them, or a ball, so that they could have spent the better part of the day here. They blamed one another.

"You, Nandini!" said Rajeshwari. "You never plan ahead!"

"I don't!" said Nandini. "I told Parvati yesterday that . . ." Parvati stared abstractedly at her nails; then she began to plait her rather unwieldy hair. After she'd finished, she insisted she plait Nandini's hair, which she began to, admiring it at the same time. "I wish I had your hair," she said, "so straight and simple." A little later, they began to walk again, towards a higher slope. They didn't know how long they'd walked, but it became noticeably cooler, and they came to a clearing where there was no shade. There, on a rock, in front of a hilltop covered with snow, a figure was sitting by himself, looking rather small and alone, completely still but for the cobras stirring about him. The girls hesitated, not wishing to intrude, because the figure was unkempt and seemed somewhat threatening, although there was no fence indicating this was private property. At the same time, Kama was hovering semi-nakedly in mid-air, without a single tree to hide behind, hoping to take correct aim. Parvati had advanced a little more than the other two, partly out of curiosity, to see if the man was a hermit, and she was the first to be struck, in the breast, by the arrow. She experienced an instant of discomfort, and then, oddly, she found this untidy man to be far more interesting than she'd first thought, and, almost immediately, she realized he wasn't a hermit, but the Destroyer of the Universe. "So this is what he does all day," she thought, feeling strangely protective towards the considerably older man. Meanwhile, Kama, after much procrastination and introspection, and weighing the dubious good and certain trouble that would come of this act, especially to him, released the second arrow, resignedly. Immediately, Shiv opened his eyes and, seeing the approaching Parvati, felt what every member of the male sex feels at one point or another, from the fourteen-year-old boy daydreaming or staring surreptitiously at a picture, to self-respecting pillars of society, although, admittedly, it had taken Shiv a much longer time to experience this than most others. Enraged at the interruption of his meditation, he looked at Kama. Kama felt an unpleasant tingling near his toes, going up to his head; and then he turned to ashes. His bow fell with a heavy, muffled sound to the ground.

A few days later, finding her daughter listless and thin, Parvati's mother asked her, "What's the matter, Paro, not feeling well?" Parvati shook her head; her eyes were small with sleeplessness. "If there's something worrying my daughter, she can tell me, you know," her mother said gently. Parvati looked at the floor; she said nothing. "Can't I get a word out of you?" said her mother, pretending to be hurt. "If you can't trust your mother, who can you . . ." Parvati said, "Mother, there's nothing wrong," angrily; and the next moment, crying a little, said, "I can't tell you about it!" Now her mother attempted to bribe her and plead with her, ran her hand through her hair and massaged her arms, until Parvati finally admitted she wanted to marry and, on further obdurate prodding, said the word "Shiv." Immediately, the palace went into mourning, as if a great calamity had occurred; loud wails were heard, and not everyone, in the midst of the noise, knew what the fuss was about. Eventually, Himalaya came to see his daughter; not so much to confront her, as to reason with her.

"Parvati, what's this I'm hearing?" said the king. "I can't believe that what I hear is true." He was a short, squat man with a beard, with hair coming down to a little below his shoulders. "I know you to be a sensible girl." Parvati deployed silence to indicate that what he'd heard was true.

"He can't make you happy," said her father. "He's unclean, temperamental, and generally not fit for polite society."

"He is," said Parvati coldly, "the Destroyer of the Universe."

"I don't care what he is," said Himalaya, equally cold. "I haven't met him, but I've heard of him—of his damru, and his tiger skins, and his third eye. I know of far better suitors for you. As far as I know, he doesn't even have any possessions, and he doesn't seem to intend to acquire any. You'll have to sleep on the floor, you know, if you marry him."

Meanwhile, Shiv was sitting with the nandi bhringi, his cohorts, and smoking a round of ganja. The cheroots flickered in the dark. There was an air of tempered happiness and sadness in the congregation, not unmixed with nostalgia, that these quiet intervals of camaraderie and introspection should be about to end, and a sweet expectancy at the wedding. Someone, absently, began to hum a tune, not very melodiously.

"There'll be glitter and there'll be shehnai," said one, who was lying on his back. "There'll be payesh and yoghurt."

Himalaya sighed as well; he'd been unable to persuade his daughter. How could he get out of this one? Then to give his daughter away to that . . . that . . . He'd always visualized the wedding as a grand occasion.

White Lies

HE RANG THE DOORBELL ONCE, and waited for the door to open. It was an ornate door, with a rather heavy, ornamental padlock. When the old, smiling maidservant opened it, there was a narrow corridor behind her that revealed a large hall and further rooms inside, like shadows contained in a prism.

It was a particularly beautiful flat. He sat on the sofa, as the maidservant went inside and said, "Memsaab, guruji aaye hai." He glanced at the Arabian Sea and Marine Drive outside; and then looked at the brass figure of Saraswati, from whose veena all music is said to emanate, on one end of a shelf. When ten minutes had passed, he briefly consulted his watch, its hands stuck stubbornly to their places, and then desultorily opened a copy of *Stardust*. Now and again, he hummed the tune of a devotional.

After another five minutes, a lady emerged, her hair not yet quite dry. "Sorry Masterji," she said, but, glancing quickly over

her shoulder, was clearly more concerned about the "fall" of her
sari.

The "guruji" shifted uncomfortably. Although he was, indeed, her guru (and without the guru, as the saying goes, there is
no knowledge), he had also the mildly discomfited air of a
schoolboy in her presence and in this flat: this had to do not
only with the fact that she was older, but with the power people
like her exercised over people like him.

"That's all right, behanji," he said; from the first day, she had
been his "respected sister." "We'll have less time for the lesson
today, that's all," he said, chuckling, but also asserting himself
subtly. Then, to placate her, he said quickly, "Maybe I arrived a
little early."

This morning was quiet, except for the activity in the
kitchen that indicated the essentials were being attended to. In
the bedroom, next to the huge double bed, the harmonium had
already been placed on the carpet by the bearer, John. The air
inside had that early-morning coolness where an air conditioner
has not long ago been switched off.

"A glass of thanda paani," he said after sitting down. This request materialised a couple of minutes later, the glass of cold
water held aloft on a plate by John, while Mrs. Chatterjee
turned the pages of her songbook unhurriedly, glancing at bhajan
after bhajan written in her own handwriting. They were too high
up—on the fourteenth floor—to hear the car horns or any of the
other sounds below clearly; the sea was visible from the windows, but too distant to be audible. Sometimes her husband,
Mr. Chatterjee, would be present—and he'd shake his head
from time to time, while sitting on the bed, listening to the guru
and his wife going over a particular phrase, or line. Sometimes
he was content doing this even while taking off his tie and waiting for tea, his office-creased jacket recently discarded on the
bed, beside him.

Indeed, he had married her twenty-two years ago for this very reason: that he might hear her sing continually. Not everyone might agree about the enormity of her talent; but something had touched him that day when he'd met her in the afternoon in his still-to-be in-laws' place in one of the more distant reaches of a small town, and heard her sing, not the usual Tagore song, but a Hindi devotional by Meerabai. He was the "catch" then—a medium-sized fish that had the potential to be a big one.

Fifteen years they'd lived together in Bombay now, and for ten years in this flat that gave the illusion from certain angles that the sea approached very near it. And for fifteen years, almost, he had wanted his wife's voice to be heard more widely than it was—what he thought of as "widely" was a hazy audience comprising mainly colleagues from his company, and from the many other companies he had to infrequently, but repeatedly, come into contact with—though it wasn't as if he'd mind terribly if the audience extended beyond this group of semi-familiar faces into the unclear territory of human beings outside.

She had a weak voice, admittedly. It managed one and a half octaves with some difficulty; it was more at ease in the lower register, but quavered when it reached the upper sa and re, something the guru had grown used to. When she sang "Meera ke prabhu" now, towards the end of the song, there was, again, that quaver. It was something she met reasonably bravely, head-on, or ignored it altogether, as did the guru. Neither could continue their respective pursuits—she, of being a singer, he, of being her teacher—if they took the quaver and its signal too seriously; they knew that one or two of these limitations were irremediable, but without much significance in relation to the other dimensions of their partnership.

"How was that?" she asked after she'd finished. She needed to know, in a perfunctory but genuine way, his opinion.

"It was all right today," he said. He was never quite ingratiating in his response, but never harshly critical, either. They had reached a silent mandate that this was how it should be. He went over a phrase as the servant brought in a tray with teacups and a small plate of biscuits.

It was always a pleasure to hear him, even when he was humming, as he was now. And he was always humming. There was no denying his gift; but he probably still didn't quite know what to do with it. He was almost careless with it. He sipped the tea slowly and carefully selected a biscuit. Sometimes they might give him a gulab jamun, towards which he'd show no lack of intent or hesitation, or a jalebi.

HE WAS CERTAINLY NOT the first teacher she'd had. He was the latest in a line that went back these fifteen years; he'd arrived to take his place at the head of the line, and to succeed his predecessors, roughly sixteen or seventeen months ago. She had interviewed him, of course, or conducted a little audition in the sitting room, during which she'd asked him, respectfully, to "sing something." He had descended on the carpet self-consciously, between the glass table and the sofas, and enchanted her, humbly but melodiously, with a bhajan she couldn't remember having heard before. She shook her head slowly from side to side to denote her acknowledgement of his prowess, and his ability to touch her, and because she hadn't heard anyone sing quite so well in a long time; and yet it *was* an interview, at the end of which there was a silence; and then she said: "Wah! Very good!"

At first, she'd called him "Masterji" (which she still did at times), as she had all her former teachers. There was no formal, ceremonial seal on the relationship, as there is between guru and shishya; he was there to do his job, to be a teacher, and she to learn. Nevertheless, the relationship had its own definition. They'd grown dependent on each other; he, for the modicum of respect he received here (fit enough for a guru, even though he might be a mere purveyor of knowledge rather than a repository of it), and the by no means negligible amount he got paid; there were also the little ways in which Mr. Chatterjee helped him out, with his official contacts. As for Mrs. Chatterjee, she liked the tunes he set the bhajans to, and could also recognise the presence of accomplishment; and she was too tired to look for another teacher. She used to change teachers every three or four years, when they began to dominate her too much; or when they became irregular. But he was much younger than she, and she'd grown fond of him—he was very mild and had none of the offensive manners that gurus sometimes have; she'd come to call him "Masterji" less and less, and addressed him, increasingly, as "Mohanji" or "Mohan bhai."

MR. CHATTERJEE CAME HOME at a quarter to seven, and called out to his wife, "Ruma!"

Later they had tea together in the balcony, facing Marine Drive and watching the sun set at seven-thirty, because it was late summer. Everywhere the glow of electricity became more apparent as the swathe of pink light permeating the clouds above the sea slowly disappeared; now darkness, and with it an artificial nocturnal light, was coming to this part of Bombay.

"Sometimes I feel we have so much, Ruma," Mr. Chatterjee sighed. She didn't know what he meant; she didn't even know if it was a complaint or an uncharacteristic confession of gratitude. Of course it wasn't true; that was obvious—they didn't have children. Towards the beginning, they'd tried various kinds of treatment; and then they'd given up trying without entirely giving up hope. Now, as you slowly cease to miss a person who's no longer present, they no longer missed the child they didn't have. They gave themselves to their lives together.

"We should go to the party by nine at least," he said. In spite of the tone of alacrity he used with his wife, the idea of having to go to the party exhausted him tonight. To change the subject, and also to allow the communion they'd had with evening to survive a little, he asked:

"What did he teach you today? A new bhajan?" Today was Thursday, the day the "he" in the enquiry came to the house. She thought briefly, half her mind already busying itself for the social activity ahead, for the new sari to be worn, and said:

"No, the one he gave me last week. It still needs polishing. The one about the Rana—'My Ranaji, I will sing the praises of Govind.' It's a beautiful tune."

"Well, you must sing it for me," he said, sighing as he got up from the sofa, resigned to the evening ahead. She looked at his back with a sort of indulgence.

THE SONG, which she'd once sung to a different tune, and which she'd been practising assiduously for the last ten days or so, was about how Meera had given herself from childhood to her one lord, the Lord Krishna, and couldn't bring herself to live with her husband, the Rana, the king. The Rana, said the song, sent her a cup of poison that became nectar when she touched it to her lips; if the Rana was angry, she sang, she could flee his province, but where would she go if her Lord turned against her? Mrs. Chatterjee rather liked the song; in her mind, of course, there was no confusion about who was her Rana and who her Lord. Krishna's flute was second fiddle for her, although it, too, had its allure. But its place in her life was secondary, though constant.

IN ANOTHER AGE, Mr. Chatterjee, with his professional abilities and head for figures and statutes, his commitment to see a project through, might have been a munshi in a court, or an advisor to a small feudal aristocracy. Now it was he who, in a sense, ruled; he ran a company; he was the patron as far as people like Mohanji were concerned. It didn't matter that, when he sang before him, Mr. Chatterjee didn't understand the talas, that he simply smiled quizzically and shook his head from side to side in hesitant appreciation. That hesitant appreciation, to Mohanji, meant much.

Coming back home from the party, Mrs. Chatterjee would be so tired that sometimes she fell asleep with makeup still on her face. At such times, she felt almost glad she didn't have children, because she would have lacked the energy to look in on them. All the same, she couldn't sleep for very long and was awake, although she looked as if she needed more rest, when the cleaner came in for the keys to wash their two cars. She stood near the balcony with a teacup in her hand as the day began, not really seeing the sea, its water resplendent with sunlight. Then she might remember the guru was to come that day, and begin to think of the last song she'd learnt from him.

On these days, she'd sometimes be a bit listless during the lesson, and the guru would say, "Behanji, you seem a bit tired today."

"It's this life, Mohanji," she'd say, preoccupied, but not entirely truthful in the impression she sought to give of being someone who was passively borne by it. "Sometimes it moves too quickly." And she'd recall the exchanges of the previous night, now gradually growing indistinguishable from one another. Mohanji would regard her with incomprehension and indulgence; he was used to these bursts of anxiety and lassitude; the way an evening of lights, drinks, and strangers, when she was transformed into something more than herself, should

change back into this sluggish morning, when she was unrecep-
tive to the lesson and to him.

IN THIS BUILDING ITSELF, there were other amateur
singers. On the seventh floor, Mrs. Prem Raheja sang devotion-
als. Her husband was a dealer in diamonds, and occasionally
flew to Brussels. For her, singing was less an aesthetic pastime
(as it was for Mrs. Chatterjee) than a religious one; she was de-
voutly religious. Then there was Neha Kapur on the eleventh
floor, who liked to sing ghazals. No one really knew what her
husband did; some said he was in "import-export." These people
were really traders made good, many times richer, in reality, than
Mr. Chatterjee, though they lacked his power and influence,
and inhabited a somewhat different world from his.

The guru had increased his clientele, if his students could
be called by that name, in visiting this building and this area.
Mrs. Raheja was now one among his students, as was Mrs. Kapur; and there were others in the neighbouring buildings. When
he came to this area, he usually visited two or three flats in a
day. The "students" were mainly well-to-do or even rich housewives, with varying degrees of talent and needs for assurance,
their lives made up of various kinds of spiritual and material requirements. What spiritual want he met was not clear, though it
was certain he met some need; and his own life had become
more and more dependent, materially, on fulfilling it.

Mohanji's life was a round of middle-aged women, mainly in
Colaba and Cuffe Parade, and a few in Malabar Hill; in his way,
he was proud of them, and thought of them as Mr. So-and-So's
wife or, where the surname denoted a business family, Mrs. So-
and-So. He moved about between Cuffe Parade and Malabar
Hill and the areas in between using buses and taxis, glimpsing,

from outside and within, the tall buildings, in which he ascended in lifts to arrive at his appointed tuition. This was a daily itinerary, before it disappeared, too temporarily for it to be disturbing to him, when he took the fast train to Dadar at night.

MR. CHATTERJEE'S COMPANY (although he didn't own the company, it was known among his friends as "Amiya's company" and among others as "Mr. Chatterjee's company") manufactured, besides other things, detergent, which was its most successful product; and, since the company had substantial foreign shareholdings—the word "multinational," like a term describing some odd but coveted hybrid, was being heard more and more these days—he, with his wife, made occasional trips to Europe (he to study the way detergent was marketed there), every one and a half to two years.

Upon their return, the vistas and weather of London and Zurich would stay with them for about a week as they resumed their life in Bombay. They'd distribute gifts among friends and business associates: deodorants, eau de toilettes, ties; for Mohanji, a cake of perfumed soap, polished like an egg, serrated like a shell. He, in his gentle, qualified way, would pretend to be more grateful than he was, but nevertheless wonder at this object that had travelled such a huge distance.

THERE WERE SO MANY PROJECTS inside Mr. Chatterjee's head; he had only a year to bring them to fruition. Though he was to retire, he was inwardly confident he'd get an extension.

In other ways, he felt that he was entering the twilight of his life in the company; though there was nothing more substantial than an intuition to suggest this. He suppressed this feeling before it could become a concrete thought. Among the more minor and personal, but persistent and cherished, projects he had in mind was to present his wife, Ruma, before an audience of friends and peers, with the repertoire of new songs she'd learnt from the guru. With this in mind, he'd ask her sometimes, with a degree of impatience:

"Isn't he teaching you anything new? I've been hearing the same two songs for the last three weeks!" This might be said in the midst of talking about three or four other things, after he'd returned, yet again, late from the office.

He asked the teacher the same question in the course of the week, when he happened to come back earlier than usual, and found the lesson midway, in progress. He'd had a distracting day at the office, and he was about to go out again. He said, looming in his navy blue suit over the teacher sitting on the carpet with the harmonium before him:

"Do give her another one, guruji! I've been hearing the same one—the one about 'Giridhar Gopal'—for about two weeks now." He called him "guruji" at times, not as a student or acolyte might, but to indicate a qualified respect for a walk of life he didn't quite understand. He used the term as one might use a foreign word that one was slightly uncomfortable with, but which one took recourse to increasingly and inadvertently.

The guru looked a little bemused, and embarrassed on Mr. Chatterjee's behalf. He picked up a printed songbook.

"I did give behanji a new bhajan, Chatterjee saheb," he said diffidently, but not without some humour and his characteristic courtesy. "Maybe you haven't heard it. It's a lovely tune," he said, with a kind of innocent and immodest delight in his own composing abilities.

"Really?" said Mr. Chatterjee, lowering himself upon the edge of the bed and apparently forgetting the appointment he had to keep. "Do sing it for me, guruji." He could spare five minutes. "Your behanji doesn't tell me anything!"

The guru began to sing almost immediately, first clearing his throat with excessive violence; then an unexpectedly melodious voice issued from him; he looked up, smiling, twice at Mr. Chatterjee while singing.

"Wah!" said Mr. Chatterjee with unusual candour after the guru finished, the song fading in less than three minutes. He turned to his wife and asked, "Have you picked it up?" She waved him away with an admonitory gesture of the hand. "See? She doesn't listen to anything I say." The guru was greatly amused at this untruth. On his way out, Mr. Chatterjee looked into the room and said, "It's a particularly lovely bhajan."

The guru smiled, almost as if he were a child who'd entered forbidden territory; as if, through the bhajan, he'd entered a space, and a mind, generally reserved for official appointments and more weighty transactions than these; how else could he obtrude upon such a space?

TWO MONTHS LATER they had a party in the flat; it came in the wake, ostensibly, of a new diversification for the company, but it actually had little to do with that. There were parties every two weeks, sometimes for no good reason, except to satisfy the addiction to the same set of faces; though these events were justified as being necessary for off-duty chatter among colleagues and associates and, more important, because there was a persuasive myth that it was an extension of business activity. Usually, however, the party turned out to be none of these, but an occasion for bad jokes, bickering, and mild drunkenness and indigestion.

This party was a little different, though; Mrs. Chatterjee was to sing tonight. Of course, she could be found standing by the door, a weak smile on her face, responding to the exclamations of "Ruma!" and "Mrs. Chatterjee!" and "Where's Amiya?" as guests walked in with little nods and smiles, half her mind on the kitchen. They didn't know yet that she was to be a prima donna that evening; going in, however, they noticed a harmonium and tablas kept on one of the carpets, and continued to circulate loudly among themselves, exploding noisily at moments of hilarity.

No one was surprised, or took more than a cursory note of the instruments; "musical evenings" were less and less uncommon these days, and were seen to be a pleasant diversion or a necessary hazard in polite society. Meanwhile, people cupped potato wafers and peanuts like small change in their hands; and a platter of shami kababs passed from person to person. The guru had come earlier, and was sitting with members of his family—his wife, his mother, his cousin, a shy and thin man who'd play the tabla today, and his son—cloistered in the air-conditioned guest room, semi-oblivious of the noise outside; they were having their own party, chattering in their own language, holding glasses of Limca or Fanta in their hands, unmindful of the party outside.

Mrs. Chatterjee hardly had time to think of the songs she'd rehearsed; she went frequently to the kitchen, her face pale, to see how the pulao was coming along, and to leave a regulatory word or two with the servants, whom she could never trust entirely. As she checked to see if the right cutlery was out, and the correct arrangement of crockery, a ghost of a tune hovered in the back of her head. She wasn't really missed; one was missed at other people's parties, but not at one's own; one was not so much the centre of attention at one's own as a behind-the-scenes worker. Other people became centres of attention, like the advertising man, Baig, who was holding forth now about the travails of advertising in a "third-world country." Yet forty-five minutes later, leaving the kitchen on autopilot, she had to suffer herself to be, briefly, the cynosure of all eyes.

The cook measured out the koftas, while, in the hall, Mrs. Chatterjee lowered herself awkwardly on the carpet, the guru sitting down not far away from her, unobtrusively, before the harmonium. He looked small and intent next to her, in his white kurta and pyjamas, part accompanist and part—what? At first, it wasn't the guests who listened to them, but they who listened, almost attentively, to the sound the guests made, until whispers travelled from one part of the room to another, the hubbub subsided, and the notes of the harmonium became, for the first time, audible. Mohanji could hear the murmurs, in English, of senior executives who worked in twenty-storey buildings nearby, and knew more about takeovers than music; it must be a puzzling, but oddly thrilling, experience to sing for them. It was odd, too, to sit next to Mrs. Chatterjee, not as if he were her guru (which he wasn't, not even in name), waiting for her to begin, indispensable but unnoticed. The guests were looking at her.

She began tentatively; she couldn't quite get hold of the first song, but no one noticed. Certainly, Mr. Chatterjee looked relaxed and contented. The only doubt was on Mrs. Chatterjee's own face; the second one, however, went off better than the first. "You're a lucky guy," said Motwane, a director in a pharmaceuticals company, prodding Mr. Chatterjee in the shoulder from behind. "I didn't know she had so many talents." Mr. Chatterjee smiled, and waved at another friend across the room. Now, in the third song, her voice faltered in the upper register, but no one seemed to hear it, or, if they did, to be disturbed. Once her performance was over, the shami kababs were circulated again; a faint taste of "culture" in their mouths, people went to the bar to replenish their glasses.

THAT NIGHT, as they were getting into bed, Mr. Chatterjee said, "That went quite well." It wasn't clear to what he was referring at first, but it was likely he meant the party itself. Mrs. Chatterjee was removing her earrings. "And the songs?" she asked pointedly, making it sound like a challenge, but only half serious.

"Those were nice," he said. To her surprise, he began to hum a tune himself, not very melodiously—she couldn't tell if it was one of the songs she'd sung earlier—something he did rarely before others, although she'd heard him singing in the bathroom, his voice coming from behind the shower. He seemed unaware that anyone else was listening. Seeing him happy in this way—it couldn't be anything else—she felt sorry for him, and smiled inwardly, because no one, as he was so successful, ever felt sorry for him, or thought of his happiness.

"We must have one of these 'musical evenings' again," he said simply, following an unfinished train of thought, as if he were a child who spoke impulsively, trusting to intuition. Yet, if he were a child, he was one who had the power to move destinies. Not in a god-like way, perhaps, but in the short term, materially. But she loved his child-like side, its wild plans, although it tired her at times. She said nothing.

IN HIS CHILD-LIKE WAY, he could be quite hard. Not with her; but no investment justified itself to him except through its returns. That was because he couldn't run a company on charity or emotions; or his own head would roll. Nor did he believe that the country could be run on charity or emotion.

She, in the long hours that he was away, leaned more and more on the guru. It wasn't that she felt lonely; but no one leading her kind of life in that flat, her husband in the office, could help but feel, from time to time, alone. The best she could think of someone like the guru, given his background, was as a kind of younger brother, "kind of" being the operative words—not as a friend; certainly not as the guru he was supposed to be. There was one guru in her life, and that was her husband. But she needed Mohanji. She might spend a morning shopping at Sahakari Bhandar, but needed to, also, learn new songs. And yet her mind was focussed on a hundred other things as well. When her focus returned to her singing, it was sometimes calming, and sometimes not.

One day she said to him mournfully:

"I wish I could sing like you, Mohanji. There are too many parties these days. I can't practise properly." Mohanji was always surprised by the desires that the rich had, a desire for what couldn't be theirs. It also amused him, partly, that it wasn't enough for Mrs. Chatterjee that she, in one sense, possessed him; she must possess his gift as well. Perhaps in another life, he thought, not in this one. The guru was a believer in karma phal, that what you did in one life determined who and where you were in the next; he was convinced, for instance, that his gift, whatever he might have done to perfect it in this life, had been given to him because of some sadhana, some process of faith and perseverance, he had performed in an earlier one. Of course, there were advantages to the position he was in now; in another time, he'd have had to submit to the whims of a rajah, with the not inconsiderable compensation that the rajah loved music. That empathy for music was still not good enough, though, to make you forget the frustrations of living under a tyrant. Now, in this age, all he had to do was attend to the humours of executives and businessmen and their wives who thought they had a taste, a passing curiosity, for music; it was relatively painless.

"Why do you say such things, behanji," he said, unruffled. He scratched the back of his hand moodily. "There's been a lot of improvement." His eyes lit up slightly. "All those bada sahibs and their wives came up and congratulated you the other day after you sang, didn't they, behanji," he said, recalling the scene, "saying, 'Bahut achhe, Rumaji,' and 'Very nice.'" He shook his head. "If you'd come to me ten years ago, I could have . . ." He sometimes said this with a genuine inkling of accomplishment at what he might have achieved.

"They may be bada sahibs," said Mrs. Chatterjee, vaguely dissatisfied that this appellation should be given to someone else's husband. "But Mr. Chatterjee is a bigger bada sahib than all of them."

The guru did not dispute this.

"Bilkul!" he said. "Even to look at he is so different." He said this because he meant it; Mr. Chatterjee, for him, had some of the dimensions of greatness, without necessarily possessing any of its qualities. There were so many facets to his existence; so little, relatively, one could know about him.

BUT THE GURU WASN'T always well. A mysterious stomach ulcer—it was an undiagnosed ailment, but he preferred to call it an "ulcer"—troubled him. It could remain inactive for days, then come back in a sharp spasm that would leave him listless for two days. To this end he'd gone with his mother and wife to a famous religious guru called, simply, Baba, and sat among a crowd of people to receive his benediction. When his turn came, he was asked only to touch Baba's feet, and, as he did so, the Baba whispered a few words into his ear, words that he didn't understand. But after this, Mohanji felt better, and the pain, though he hadn't expected it would, seemed to go away.

When his behanji heard about this one day, she was properly contemptuous. "I don't believe in baba-vaaba," she said. The guru smiled, and looked uncomfortable and guilty; not because he'd been caught doing something silly, but because Mrs. Chatterjee could be so naively sacrilegious. It was as if she didn't feel the need to believe in anything, and affluent though she might be, the guru was not certain of the wisdom of this. "If you have a problem, it should be looked at by a *real* doctor," she went on. The guru nodded mournfully, seeing no reason to argue.

Of course, the problem was partly Mohanji's own fault. As he went from flat to flat, he was frequently served "snacks" during the lesson, the junk food that people stored in their homes and dispensed with on such occasions. Sometimes the food could be quite heavy. Mohanji could never resist these, eating them while thinking, abstractedly, of some worry that beset him at home. This irregular consumption would leave him occasionally dyspeptic.

HE SUFFERED FROM tension as well, a tension from constantly having to lie to the ladies he taught—white lies, flattery—and from not having a choice in the matter. He had raised his fee recently, of course; he now charged a hundred rupees for lessons all around, pleading that a lot of the money went towards the taxi fare. In this matter, his "students" found him quietly inflexible. "I can't teach for less," he said simply. And because he was such an expert singer, his "students" couldn't refuse him, although a hundred rupees a "sitting" was a lot for a guru; making him one of the highest-paid teachers doing the rounds. But they'd begun to wonder, now and again, what they were getting out of it themselves, and why their singing hadn't improved noticeably, or why they—housewives—couldn't also become singers with something of a reputation: it would be a bonus in the variegated mosaic of their lives.

"But you must practise," he'd say; and when a particular murki or embellishment wouldn't come to them, he'd perform a palta or a vocal exercise, saying, "Practise this: it's for that par-

ticular murki," as if he were a mountebank distributing charms
or amulets for certain ailments.

MR. CHATTERJEE'S OFFICE HAD a huge rosewood table;
now, on the third anniversary of his being made Chief Executive
of this company, a basket of roses arrived; after a couple of files
were cleared away, it was placed on a table before him, and a
photograph taken by a professional photographer arranged by
Patwardhan, the Personnel Manager. "Okay, that's enough; back
to work," he said brusquely, after the camera's shutter had
clicked a few times. Once the photograph was developed and
laminated, its black-and-white colours emphasised, rather than
diminished, the roses.

The guru loved this photograph. "Chatterjee saheb looks
wonderful in it—just as he should," he said, admiring it. "He
must have a wonderful office." He ruminated for a little while,
and said, "Brite detergent—he owns it, doesn't he, behanji?" "He
doesn't *own* it," said Mrs. Chatterjee, tolerant but short. "He
runs it." The guru nodded, not entirely convinced of the distinction.

He continued to give her new songs, by the blind poet
Surdas, and by Meera, who would accept no other Lord but
Krishna. During these lessons, he came to know, between songs,
in snatches of conversation, that Mr. Chatterjee had got his two-
year extension at the helm of the company. He took this news
home with him and related it proudly to his wife.

Two days later, he brought a box of ladoos. "These aren't from
a shop—" he pointed out importunately. "My wife made them!"
Mrs. Chatterjee looked at them as if they'd fallen from outer space.
There they sat, eight orbs inside a box, the wife's handiwork.

"Is there a festival?" asked Mrs. Chatterjee. In the background, John, the old servant, dusted, as he did at this time of the day, the curios in the drawing room.

"No, no," said the guru, smiling at her naiveté and shaking his head. "She made them for you—just eat them and see." She wasn't sure if she wanted to touch them; they looked quite rich.

"I'll have one in the evening," she consoled him. "When Chatterjee saheb comes. He'll like them with his tea." But in the evening, Mr. Chatterjee demurred.

"This'll give me indigestion," he said; but he was distracted as well. No sooner had he been given his extension than a bickering had started among a section of the directors about it; not in his presence, of course, but he was aware of it. At such times, he couldn't quite focus on his wife's music lessons, or on the guru; the guru was like a figure who'd just obtruded upon Mr. Chatterjee's line of vision, but whom he just missed seeing. "You know sweets like these don't agree with me." The sweets were an irrelevance; if the two directors—one of whom, indeed, he'd appointed himself—succeeded in fanning a trivial resentment, it would be a nuisance, his position might even be in slight danger; he must be clear about that. You worked hard, with care and foresight, but a little lack of foresight—which was what appointing Sengupta to the Board had turned out to be—could go against you. Sometimes, he knew from experience and from observing others, what you did to cement your position was precisely what led to undoing it.

Mrs. Chatterjee felt a twinge of pity for Mohanji. As if in recompense, she ate half a ladoo herself. Then, unable to have any more, she asked John to distribute them among the cook, the maidservant, and himself. "They're very good," she told them. She could see her husband was preoccupied, and whispered her instructions.

•　•　•

SENSING A TENSION for the next couple of weeks, which was unexpected since it came at the time of the extension being summoned, a time, surely, for personal celebration, she herself grew unmindful, and withdrew into conversations with a couple of friends she felt she could trust. Once or twice, the guru asked her, full of enthusiasm, what she'd thought of the ladoos, but never got a proper answer. "Oh those were nice," she said absently, leaving him hungry for praise. A slight doubt had been cast upon the extension, although it was trivial and this was most probably an ephemeral crisis; still, she felt a little cheated that it should happen now. It also made her occasionally maudlin with the guru, less interested in the lesson than in putting unanswerable questions to him.

"Mohan bhai, what's the good of my singing and doing all this hard work? Who will listen?" How quickly their moods change, he thought. There you are, he thought, with your ready-made audience of colleagues and colleagues' wives; what more do you want? The questions she'd asked chafed him, but he skirted them, like a person avoiding something unpleasant in his path. One day, however, he was feeling quite tired (because of a bad night he'd had) and lacked his usual patience; he said:

"One mustn't try to be what one can't, behanji. You have everything. You should be happy you can sing a little, and keep your husband and your friends happy. You can't be a professional singer, behanji, and you shouldn't try to be one." Mrs. Chatterjee was silenced briefly by his audacity and wondered what had made him say it. For the first time in days, she saw him through the haze of her personal anxieties; for a few moments she said nothing. Then she said:

"Perhaps you're right." Her eyes, though, had tears in them.

When Mr. Chatterjee heard of this exchange, he was very angry. In spite of all they had, he'd never felt he'd given his wife enough. And because she sang, and sometimes sang before him, it was as if she gave him back something extra in their life to-gether, and always had. It wasn't as if she had the presence or the personality or the charm that some of the wives in her posi-tion had; it wasn't as if she was an asset to the society they moved about in. Her singing was her weakness, and it was that weakness that made him love her more than he otherwise would have.

"How dare he say such a thing?" he said, genuinely out-raged. He was angry enough to forget, temporarily, the little fac-tions that had come into being in the company. "I will speak to him. As if he can get away just like that, disclaiming all respon-sibility." Without really meaning it, he added, "You can always get another teacher, you know."

Two days later, he delayed setting out for his office, and deliberately waited for the guru to arrive. Barely had the music lesson begun, and the recognisable sounds of voice and harmo-nium emerged from the room, than Mr. Chatterjee looked in, fully suited, and ready to go. The guru, seeing him, this vision of executive energy, bowed his head quickly in mid-song, privileged that the Managing Director should have stopped to listen to him for a few moments. Mr. Chatterjee was impatient today, and wasn't taking in the Surdas bhajan; he had a meeting with the Board.

"Ji saheb," said the guru, stopping.

"Guruji," said Mr. Chatterjee, "please don't say things that will upset my wife. That is not your job. You are here to give her songs and improve her singing. If you can't do that pro-perly . . ."

"What did I say, Chatterjee saheb?" asked the guru, inter-rupting him, and noticeably concerned. "Saheb, she has ten new songs now . . ."

"Don't evade the issue," snapped Mr. Chatterjee. "You told

her, didn't you, that she could never be a real singer. What is your responsibility, then? Do you take a hundred rupees a turn just to sit here and listen to her?"

The guru's hands had grown clammy. "I won't listen to such nonsense again," said Mr. Chatterjee, shutting the door behind him. "Please switch off the air conditioner, behanji," the guru said after Mr. Chatterjee had gone. "I'm feeling cold."

IT WASN'T AS IF the guru began to dislike Mr. Chatterjee after this. He took his words, in part, as a childish outburst, and they couldn't quite hurt him. One thing he understood anew was how little Mr. Chatterjee knew about music, about the kind of ardour and talent it required. But why should he? Mr. Chatterjee's lack of knowledge of music seemed apposite to his position. If he'd been a musician, he wouldn't be Mr. Chatterjee.

The guru knew that if he wasn't careful, the Chatterjees might discard him; Mrs. Chatterjee might find herself someone else. He'd also begun to feel a little sorry for her, because of what he'd said; he could have replied, perhaps, that, given the right training from early childhood, she might have been a better-known singer, or, if she'd been in the right place and at the right time, she might have become one; there had been no need to quite expose her like that.

For the following two days, Mrs. Chatterjee, going around in her chauffeur-driven car from the club to the shops in the mornings, couldn't bring herself to hum or sing even once; the driver noted her silence. She'd suddenly realised that her need to sing had been a minor delusion, that she and her husband and the world could get by without it—she hadn't been honest with herself; and no one had been honest with her. She remained polite

with the guru when he came—they'd started to watch each
other warily now, in secret—but went through the new bhajans
with him without any real involvement, glancing again and again
at her watch to see when the hour was up. Then, after a few
more days, she realised she was taking herself too seriously; the
force of the guru's words diminished, and she began to, once
more, look forward to the lesson.

MEANWHILE, MR. CHATTERJEE had dealt with the prob-
lem at his end, after making, first of all, several late-night telephone calls to some of the foreign shareholders and directors.
He had to shout to make himself heard, sometimes keeping his
wife from sleep. "Are you sure, Humphrey?" he asked, putting
the onus of responsibility on the Englishman. And then, "Yes, I
can see there's no other way . . ." Two days later, he met Sengupta, the man he'd employed four years ago, and appointed to
the Board last year, face-to-face across the large rosewood table.
"R.C.," he said, referring to him by his initials (he himself was
"A.K."—Amiya Kumar—to his colleagues), "you know why we're
here. If there was any dissatisfaction or disagreement, we could
have thrashed it out between ourselves. But that was not to be."
As if digressing philosophically, he observed, "Brite has had a
grand history, it has a present, and a future. No person is more
important than that future." Interrupting himself, he sighed.
"Anyway, I've spoken to Dick and Humphrey, and they agree
that even the project that was your undertaking is going to fold
up. It shows no signs of promise. It was a mistake." Sengupta
had said nothing so far, not because he felt he was in the wrong,
but because he thought his position, because of what he'd done
and the way he'd done it, was a weak one; changes were necessary, but he could see now that he should have gone about look-

ing for them in a more knowing way. "One thing I want to say before I resign, A.K.," interjected Sengupta, looking at the bright space outside the large glass windows, "is that I've had a wonderful few years at Brite, and I regret it couldn't be for longer. However, I don't always agree with the company's style of functioning—it's not democratic." "Companies aren't democracies, R.C.," said Mr. Chatterjee, with the exaggerated patience of a man who was getting his way. "You weren't elected to the Board, I appointed you to it. The election was a formality. Anyway, if you wanted to effect some changes, you should have waited a couple of years. You were certainly in the running." Sengupta shook his head and smiled. "I don't know about that. Some of us make it, some of us don't—it's a bit of luck and a bit of merit, and a bit of something else." He looked at his hands. "I know my opportunity won't come again; that's all right. But—another thing—I don't think our personal world should encroach upon our business world, should it? I'm a great admirer of Ruma, a simple soul, a very pure person, but do you think that those costly parties with all that music and singing are necessary?" "Social gatherings and parties have always been part of company policy; they raise its profile and perform all kinds of functions, you know that. The music came at no extra cost," Mr. Chatterjee observed firmly. R. C. Sengupta waved a hand. "You're right, you're right, of course! But the teacher, excellent singer, what's his name, I heard you were going to sponsor some show or performance to showcase him. Of course, I don't know if what I've heard . . ." Mr. Chatterjee bristled. "Who told you that? That's absolute rubbish. He teaches my wife—I think it's unfair to draw either of them into this." He paused and reflected. "An idea may have been floated at one time, as such things are, but it was revoked." He straightened some papers on the table. "I personally thought it was a good idea. More and more companies are doing it, you know. Music is a great but neglected thing, a great part of our tradition. We should extend patronage where it's due. It can do Brite no harm." He looked at his watch. "We're late for lunch," he said.

THE GURU COLLAPSED on the street, not far from his house, one afternoon, when he was on his way home. One moment he was squinting at the sun, and trying to avoid someone's shoulder brushing past him, and the next moment, almost inadvertently, without quite realising it, he'd crumpled—bent and fallen over. A few passersby and loiterers ran towards him; he was familiar to them as the one who taught music, and from the window of whose ground-floor chawl they could sometimes hear singing. He wasn't unconscious, but had had a temporary blackout; he kept saying, "Theek hai bhai, koi baat nahi, it's all right, it's fine," as they helped him up, and one of the people, a sixteen-year-old boy who knew the way to his home, insisted on accompanying him, holding him by the arm during the slow progress homeward.

"Dadiji," said the boy to Mohanji's mother, who'd been unprepared for what greeted her, "Panditji fell down. He should rest for a while." He sounded conciliatory, as if he didn't want to alarm her.

"Haan, haan, rest; I've been telling him to rest," said the mother, as Mohanji, saying, "Theek hai, beta," to his companion, lay down on the divan and put one arm across his eyes.

His wife was not at home, nor were his two children; they'd gone to visit his wife's father in another part of the city. This chawl was where he'd grown up, and where he'd also got married. His father, who was a teacher and singer himself (he'd died eleven years ago), had moved here thirty years ago, and they'd had no intention, or opportunity, to move out since. Gradually the house had come to be known in the chawl as "Panditji's house." It was here, when he was nine or ten years old, that his father had taught him kheyal and tappa and other forms of classical music.

"MOHANJI," SAID MRS. CHATTERJEE, "what happened to you?" It wasn't as if she'd been worried; it was just that she abhorred practising alone—she preferred him there when she sang.

"I don't know what happened, behanji," said the guru with a look of ingenuous puzzlement. "I fell ill."

"I heard," said Mrs. Chatterjee, nodding slightly. "Mrs. Raheja told me . . . she told me you fell down." The guru looked discomfited, as if he'd been caught doing something inappropriate. At once, he looked somewhat triumphant.

"It might be low blood pressure." She took him to her doctor—Dr. Dastur, a middle-aged physician. He saw his patients in a room on the second storey of a building in Marine Lines. Mrs. Chatterjee sat with Mohanji in a waiting room with three other patients, waiting to be called in. Half an hour later, when they went inside, Dr. Dastur greeted her with:

"Arrey Mrs. Chatterjee, how are you? How is your husband—his name is everywhere these days?"

"Dr. Dastur," she said, "this is my music teacher. He sings beautifully."

Dr. Dastur couldn't remember having seen a music teacher at close quarters before. Not that he was uninterested in music—his daughter now played Chopin's and Bach's simpler compositions on the piano—but he himself was inordinately proud of the Indian classical tradition, which he knew as little about as most of his contemporaries.

"Masterji," he said, bequeathing this title upon Mohanji in an impromptu way, "it's a pleasure meeting you."

•   •   •

DR. DASTUR PRESCRIBED HIM medication, but Mohanji didn't take the pills with any regularity. Indeed, he had an antipathy towards pills, as if they were alive. Instead he kept a photograph of his spiritual guru—the "Baba"—close to him.

He kept his blackout from his other students. The ghazal was in boom: everyone wanted to sing songs about some imminent but unrealisable beloved. Mohanji, in keeping with this, taught Neha Kapur on the eleventh floor songs by Ghalib and more recent poets; almost every week, he, sitting at his harmonium, hummed under his breath and composed a tune.

Bhajans, too, had become big business of late; women wore their best saris and diamonds and went to the concert halls to listen to the new singers. And somehow, everyone felt that they, too, could sing, and be singers, and be famous. Even Mrs. Kapur had a dream that her voice be heard. And it took so little to achieve it—a bit of money could buy one an auditorium for a night, and a "show" could be held. Even the guru had come to believe in the simplicity of this rather uncomplicated faith.

Although he was keeping indifferent health, he'd begun to sing more and more at businessmen's mehfils, and wedding parties; someone, moved by his singing, might come up to him in the middle of a song and shyly but passionately press a hundred-rupee note to his hand. Unaccounted-for money circulated in these gatherings; they were different from the parties in the corporate world, but, in a way, these people, always ostentatious with both money and emotion, seemed to care more for the music and, moved by the pathos of some memory, shook their heads from side to side as he sang his ghazals.

•   •   •

THESE MEHFILS lasted late into the night, and sometimes Mohanji and the members of his family who'd accompanied him would return home in a taxi at two or half past two in the morning. Late night, and the heat of the day would have gone, and they'd be sleepy and exhausted but still know they were a thousand rupees richer. By this time, the housewives who'd also heard him sing would be setting aside their large gold necklaces and yawning and going to bed.

This year, when the ghazal was in boom, had been a better year than most for the guru. He'd gone round from home to home, patiently teaching new songs to housewives about the wave of long hair and sudden gestures and sidelong glances, singing at small baithaks, or even bhajans at temples before Sindhi businessmen if they so demanded it. But this would leave him tired and moody when he visited Mrs. Chatterjee. She couldn't decide whether he was unhappy for some personal reason, or because he still hadn't made a name as some other singers had.

AS THE GURU'S HEALTH WORSENED, he began to sleep more and more of the time. Sometimes the phone might ring in his small room, and he might speak for a few moments to a student who was enquiring after where he was. When he made the effort to go into the city, he slept on the train, carried along by its rhythm; and sometimes Mrs. Chatterjee, finding him tired, would feel sorry for him and let him fall asleep after a lesson on one of the wicker sofas on the balcony, overlooking the Arabian Sea and the office buildings on Nariman Point. As he rested, she might be getting ready to go out, once her husband returned, for dinner. Now and again, she'd go to the verandah to check on the guru; she would put her hand on his forehead, shake her head well-meaningly, and say, "No fever." She would glance towards the traffic on Marine Drive, because it was from that direction that her husband would be approaching.

At such times, the guru was like a pet, or a child, left to himself and intermittently tended to. As Mrs. Chatterjee and her husband prepared to go out they would talk about him as if he were a child they were leaving behind. Occasionally, if he heard her humming a song he'd taught her as she went out, he'd open his eyes, smile slightly, and close them again.

E-Minor

This city keeps growing, reconfiguring
itself; I came to it three and a half decades ago—
Kipling wrote of it as daybreak, colour,
and palm trees, ayahs. We came from Calcutta,
then the greater city. My father found a job
in a British company whose head office, like us, moved to
    Bombay.
We were put up at the Taj. This hotel's appearance
is the outcome of its architect's mistake. Commissioned
to create a facsimile of the Taj, he made
its front entrance face the city, its rear the sea.
It should have been the other way round; the entrance
we use is actually the rear; the Taj,
turned inside out, faces the city, which turns
its back to it, and the sea, looking upon

its back, won't recognise it. The architect's long dead—only
in the afterlife of his fancy do replica and original
become one, and city and building, reality, conception,
readjust themselves, to become as they're not.
There are many Bombays; this is one of them.
We spent two nights at the Taj; the fried pomfret
gave me a bad stomach (I was one and a half);
my mother panicked. I can imagine her, combative,
cradling a sick infant inside that hotel room.
For many years, she'd think of that fried pomfret
with dismayed wonder. She was glad to leave
for the company's furnished flat. For a while, in her new home,
she couldn't find a cook who would suit her, so
interviewed impostor after impostor, a few of whom

she still remembers, as if they press upon her,
and bother her with their lies and evasions. My father
had come to Bombay after spending twelve years
in England, six of them with my mother. He had
overcome a fallow period, and, with her help,
now swotting at home, now drinking tea at Lyons,
passed the exams that would give him the grand letters
next to his name. He's a chartered accountant,
and a member of the Institute of Taxation, and a Company
Secretary. These laurels gave him a job
as Assistant Company Secretary of Britannia Biscuits
Company, or BBC. This firm,
whose jobs were among the best in the "private sector,"
was still largely British-owned, a subsidiary

of Huntley & Palmer's, and Peak Freens. My father started
as a student of English; he had an Honours degree
in English Literature from Calcutta University. He changed

direction later, and went on to study
accountancy; came back from England and took
this job as an expert on taxation law.
Once or twice, I've heard him quote, "Heard melodies are
    sweet,
but those unheard are sweeter," a little self-consciously.
When I decided to study English, he was pleased. It was a
    choice
that might have bewildered other parents, but he
had ample warning. Meanwhile, biscuits
dominated our shelves. I never ate them.
Bourbon, Cream-cracker, Nice, I was familiar
with them all, but rarely touched them. I suspected,

during teatimes, that this was not the kind of food
our country needed. I rather wished
my father made bridges, or engines, or ingots,
anything instead of the round things with jam centres—
the only biscuits I liked. (Such are the whims
of fate, or whatever force binds destinies
together, that the woman who is my wife
is, as my mother puts it, a "biscuit junky."
She dips her Marie in tea; the dipped bit tans,
and, moistened, the biscuit droops like a Dalí clock.
Thus biscuits recur in my life, long after
my father's retirement, as if they were
reminding me of something.) Both my parents come from
    Sylhet,
which went to East Pakistan in 1947,

after a referendum; Sylhetis still blame Bordoloi,
then Chief Minister of Assam, for agreeing to the demand
for one. Sixteen years later, they found

—they, who'd known each other since childhood—themselves
in Khar, then in Cumballa Hill, and,
in 1971, in a flat—three bedrooms—
on the twelfth floor of a new building called
Il Palazzo ("the palace") on Malabar Hill.
This building transcended the others, so that our flat
hung midway over the Arabian Sea
and watched the Queen's Necklace from a vantage point
it would not have been possible to cheaply occupy.
For many days, the smell of new paint
hung like a benison on the flat, while shelves

and tables still not arrived at their final shape
had their naked wood whittled away by workmen.
That first night we came to the flat, those unfinished
chairs and tables and that first coat of paint
on the walls greeted us. To write about it in verse
is to make palpable to myself the experience
of living in that apartment, the pauses
and caesuras between the furniture, the dining
room, the overhanging balcony, the sea outside;
my father, recently made Finance Director, my mother,
like children gazing into a doll's house. Sylhet,
no longer memory, nor country, but just themselves.
(Sylhet, from where it's claimed, Sri Chaitanya's
parents came to Nabadweep. There, the holy child

played in the dust on all fours in the courtyard
of their home, watched by his mother. Old songs
call him the "fair moon"; this was before he grew up
and became a wanderer.) Outside our balcony,
too, a fair moon hovered that night. Sylhet—

aeons of migration; even now, most of the
Indian restaurants in England are run by Sylheti
Muslims: the menu's a delirious poem
on which the names of Moghlai and Punjabi and Parsi
dishes—chicken korma, bhuna meat, dhansak—
are placed in a proximity they'll never be in elsewhere.
Relocated twice; the first time, when Bengal
was broken up in 1905, and Sylhet annexed
to Assam. When my father was a student in Calcutta,

a man from Chittagong said to him in his hostel:
"Sylhet? So you're from Assam! Don't you eat humans there?"
My father said: "Yes, we do. Do drop in for lunch."
In Il Palazzo, the transition was made
from humans to biscuits. There were cut-glass ashtrays
collected from Denmark, placed strategically
in a non-smoking house (my father's one or two
attempts at a social cigar have left him ill),
guarded on all sides by a regiment of curios.
Those ashtrays populated my childhood like unusable toys.
Of course, we knew this life, refracted
through cut glass, reflected on brass, was, in part,
make-believe—even I, as a child, knew it—that
the furniture, the flat, weren't ours. Yet that view,

morning and evening, of the Arabian Sea
and the Queen's Necklace, and the dome of the Taj,
was all mine. At that time, I was more
interested in prying into windows of the buildings
not too far away—I had a pair of binoculars
given me by a friend of my father's from England
that took me near those rooms, and, looked into from

the wrong lenses, gave me the strange satisfaction
of feeling farther away than I really was.
I knew our country was poor, but mainly as a
sombre abstraction. Having said that, our wealth
was make-believe—perquisites (perks) made up
for the ceiling on high income under Indira Gandhi.

My father had no savings—he'd lost everything
with partition; the take-home pay, after tax,
was small. The only way to get rich was not to pay
taxes, almost impossible to do when you had
one of the best jobs available in a British-owned company.
But the perquisites gave us the trappings of affluence
if not affluence itself. A chauffeur-driven car,
first an Ambassador, then a "foreign" car,
a poor relation of the Managing Director's Pontiac—
an Austin that tried to keep us happy, and often
stopped for no reason on Marine Drive. It was
often pushed into motion by passersby. Domiciled
in India, its habits had become Indian. Still,
it *was* a foreign car (the word "foreign" had,
for the urban upper middle class,

as much a shameless magic as it might have had
a malign resonance to a nationalist or to
a Little Englander); commensurate with my father's
position. Years later, a Mercedes-Benz,
regal in those years of austerity, took us
everywhere. Wherever we went in it, we were
saluted. These cars—our cars—of varying
degrees of majesty, were not our own. (When my father
retired, he bought a secondhand Ambassador
at a concession from the company. The new

Managing Director's son had practised on it
and perfected his driving skills, permanently
affecting its engine. The chauffeur who'd driven
the Mercedes-Benz, a fair, round-faced, moustached,

uxurious Hindi-speaking man, forever dropping
his wife's name in his conversations, wept when he bid us
farewell. An age had ended for him.
He had a new employer now. A better job—
and yet these illogical tears.) That Austin
used to be parked outside the old building on
Cumballa Hill, near the Parsi General
Hospital. It was from here I went to school,
going down the road past the Allah Beli café
where drivers ate biryani for lunch—always plotting
how not to go to school, because I hated it,
hated the hymns in the morning, the P.E. classes,
physics and mathematics; plotting, feigning fever

and malingering in order to stay at home.
The fifteen or so minutes I had in the car
before I reached school near Mahatma Gandhi Road,
going past, every morning, Marine Drive, before turning
either into the road that ran past Parsi
Dairy Farm, and the Fire Temple, then right
again towards Metro Cinema, or farther on,
turning left at Churchgate, moving towards
the traffic lights before Flora Fountain—those fifteen
minutes I spent in apprehension and prayer.
It was Christ I prayed to, to save me from
the imminent danger of P.E. classes.
His power and efficacy had been impressed on me
by a series of Roman Catholic drivers,

one of whom took me to the church on Wodehouse
Road when I was seven or eight. I kept
the card-sized picture he'd given me, in which
Christ looked like a blond sixties flower child,
his face and blue eyes tilted slightly towards heaven.
It was this image I prayed to, going down Marine Lines,
or stuck in a traffic jam in Kemp's Corner. I found
a good excuse not to do P.E.—the murmur
that the stethoscope had discovered when I was three years old.
My parents took me from doctor to doctor; at first
diagnosed as a hole in the heart, then an obstruction
to a valve. My blood whispered loudly
with my heartbeat. I watched as the others touched their toes,
or executed a somersault on the "horse";

or hung, primate-like, from the Roman rings,
and thanked the Almighty I had the means to convince
my mother to write a note: "Please excuse my son
from P.E. today." School, then, was a place
of lonely observances, where a role was already
created, of watching from the sidelines; meanwhile,
we'd moved to the apartment on Malabar Hill.
The solitary quest for the other had started
long ago; the first desire was for
myself. As a child, I'd often stare
at my body in the mirror, in the silence, appraising,
weighing, sometimes touch the mirror, feeling the pleasure
was mine, but that I was being pleasured as well;
that private feeling of separateness

and connection. Later, I began to compose the secret
object of my search from odds and ends, nipples
and navels; sometimes a woman in a bikini, alone

in an advertisement; sometimes, without knowing it, the gods
and goddesses in my father's *Outline of Art*;
gods more than goddesses—as if I was still searching
for myself—the mirror, in this case,
was the picture of the gods. I flicked the pages. For a long
time the mirror stage lasted, and those Roman bodies
were touched by the hue of my skin, by my sweat,
by sameness and its odd allure. I saw a print
of a painting of Saint Sebastian, his arched torso
pierced by arrows. I couldn't distinguish
between the sacred and the profane, the spiritual passion

from the carnal. These gods were among
the earliest pornographic pictures I beheld.
The hardbound books in my father's library; besides
those on industrial growth, and development,
and fiscal policy, and the World Bank,
were the Grolier Classics—relics of his love
of prosody and line—the *Divine Comedy*,
and *Paradise Lost*, long unopened, but whose titles
spoke worlds. I thought *Paradise Lost* a tropical island;
the *Divine Comedy* a farce. Among the books
was a consumptively thin and freckled copy
of T. S. Eliot's *Selected Poems*, bought
for a shilling and sixpence in London, and shipped
more than a decade ago with other Pelican books to India.

Looking into it when I was twelve or thirteen,
I remember the bemusement and distaste
I felt, more than if I'd come upon an obscenity,
on reading the lines "I grow old . . . I grow old . . .
I shall wear the bottoms of my trousers rolled . . ."
and experiencing a great, if temporary, disillusionment,

as if some taboo had been breached. Thus, my childhood.
Never quite happy at school, never
doing as well as expected, but not
too badly either, frequently visiting
my father's office at Nariman Point, where the blinds
kept the sun out of his room. Nariman Point
didn't exist when I was very small, except as a strip
of land darkly petering out from Marine Drive

into the sea. The sea—the prisoner and attendant
god of this city, one of the points where its secular
locutions, its advertisement hoardings, its hotels,
are linked to the horizon; emptiness. Each year
we'd watch as the road congealed with people and cars,
and Ganesh was carried out to sea, the giant god
sinking, his trunk tranquil, with the Queen's Necklace
behind him, and the Cream Centre; Malabar Hill
and Walkeshwar on one side as he drowned.
The promise that he'd return next year was made good
in the same emphatic way. These days, the traffic
from Haji Ali to Peddar Road to Marine Drive to Cuffe
Parade is so bad, with massed, uncertain files
of slowly moving cars, that it seems the Ganesh festival

is perpetually in progress. Sometimes it takes an hour
to get from Haji Ali to Nariman Point. When I was
a child, it took fifteen or twenty minutes from home
in Malabar Hill, past Churchgate, to school, which began
at half past eight sharp. There were four branches: infant,
junior, middle, senior. The day began with
"Almighty Father, who art in heaven" and hymns
like "All Things Bright and Beautiful."
And though things were largely beautiful and bright

for us, the pupils, perhaps they weren't for the teachers,
who couldn't be too well paid. As for us, we were princelings
or delinquents; however poor our report cards, whatever
the black marks against our names, the blot on the pages
of our exercise books, our almighty fathers, in the end,

would save us. I had my own school diary
with the school logo on the cover; its last pages
came to be thick with the teachers' messages in the red
ink of their ballpoint pens. These admonitions
I needed to get initialled in my mother's impatient hand.
Some of the teachers vacillated between resentment
and a cold, tranquil estimate of our fathers' wealth.
Some of the very teachers who pulled us up in class
gave us private tuition for extra money.
They seemed transformed, smaller, entering our homes,
as we must have been transformed in their eyes
when they discovered our houses firsthand. A few
commanded respect naturally; but we, in reality,
commanded them all, because we could

escape them, but not they us. Repeating themselves,
possibly until the end of their working days,
they'd stand in the morning as the Lord's Prayer was said,
or write out sums, later, on the blackboard,
till the peon rang the bell; a new set of boys go home
in big cars, while teachers arrive next morning
on buses and scooters. Pigeons, their silly murmurs,
I remember from the senior school classrooms.
I recall little from all I learnt: H_2O,
NO_2, zygotes, amoebae, the life cycle
of the parasite, a ball expanding with heat
and failing to pass through a ring, the way a tinder

burst brightly into flames, thrust in a jar of oxygen,
before the flame went out, exhaling carbon dioxide.

All that comes back: the way we were looking
not at the flames, but at the freckles on the prettiest
girls' legs, at the back of their heads, and how
quickly we'd forgotten the prayers said earlier
that morning, and shrugged off fear of sin. We were
afraid of no higher entity, at least
not afraid enough. No wonder, then, after
all those hours in the classroom, we learnt so little.
There was no guardian to review our daydreams;
with the wanton abandon that belongs
to a state of natural anarchy, our imagination,
possessed by something like the whooping courage of the pillaging
soldier touring razed villages, chose the girl
two rows from us, as the lesson progressed, or even

the teacher with chalk on her fingers,
the outline of her breasts visible in the dull,
electric glow of our vision, stopping short only
at some revered and long cherished figure, like a tea taster
coming to a halt in his quick tasting, and wrinkling
his nose at something inadmissible or fundamentally wrong.
There was no VHP to monitor these pictures
in our head; there were only our parents; they couldn't know
much of what were loosely called our "thoughts." If they'd ever
had, once, similar ones themselves, they'd forgotten,
with the amnesia that growing up induces, erasing forever
what it means not to have been adult. The classes

were interspersed with the granddaughters
and grandsons of the Birlas and the Tatas, of the families

that owned Roger's soda—a scion, Pheroze,
was a close accomplice in the third standard—
and Duke's Mangola. Biscuits, soft drinks, aerated
water circulated between class and the home.
So much money in a single classroom,
albeit incarnated in the figures of children
between four and five feet tall (the taller boys pushing
the shorter ones, whenever they could, like bulls)—
if a teacher had thought to hold a classroom
to ransom, he might have recovered
enough money to recompense him for his labours
several pensions over. When promoted to the eighth

standard, I was moved from section A to section
B, where unruly students were consigned,
by a teacher, Punoose, who saw this as
a punishment for my talkativeness.
Punoose was bespectacled, overweight; we disposed
of the "Mrs." when referring to her, as a way
of cutting her to size in our conversations.
Even here, in B, there was a Birla granddaughter,
a fair, frail girl, without distinction in studies,
passably pretty, whom you'd find difficult
to associate with that industrial empire.
She had a crush on Suresh, a gymnast
and boxer, who became our contemporary because
he'd failed and had to repeat a class

(not for the first time). Finding myself seated next to him,
we argued but became friends of a kind. Shirkers
and hoodlums outnumbered angels around me; and I,
a shy—if intermittently talkative—boy,
felt obliged to pose as a hoodlum.

Thus, I got away with the grudging respect of the likes
of Arun Kapoor, whom Lobo, the physics teacher,
called "monster," not only because of his size, but for
his one stone eye. There was one brilliant boy
in that menagerie: Subramaniam. This lanky South Indian
from an unremarkable middle-class family used words
like "trepidation" and "verisimilitude."
He was chasteningly good at science: I once
visited him in his flat—a typical government-service

residence, with its large hall and sparse
furniture, and a smell of spices everywhere.
I watched as his mother brought him a tumbler of milk
and toasted sandwich. He told me, as he ate, that he ran
two miles around the undulating paths
of Altamount Road each morning. Once,
he came to *my* flat and stood before
the series of encyclopaedias on my shelves
that my father had bought me, and said, with the slightest
hint of irony and envy, and only
the remotest suggestion of judgement:
"Do you ever *read* these?" I prevaricated
guiltily; he didn't wait for my reply
but picked one up and went through its pages

intently, as if he'd consume them in a glance.
I'm sure he must be in America,
and that tenacity, which took him running two miles
in the morning, probably got him somewhere at last.
As for me, I took my chances with teachers and exams.
I kept long hair; let my mind wander;
was reprimanded, and yet I managed
to keep afloat. Suresh, who was never expected

to shine in studies, blemished his record further
by refusing to participate in competitive sports
and antagonising his house master, Lewis, the maths teacher,
for whom such things mattered. Suresh had become
a compulsive daydreamer, sitting
on the first row to the left, next to the large, sweet,

but dim Yugoslav beauty, Biljana Obradovic.
He was short but good-looking, with a hooked nose and a
    slouch,
attractive to girls. Sujata Birla's attentions
were a source of discomfiture ("She walks funny"), but he
    liked
Rehab Barodawalla, and the way, by late
morning, her socks would settle into two rings
at the bottom of her ankles. Later, in junior college,
we met again, but our interest in each other
had waned. I, for one, had become more "poetic."
I could grow my hair as long as I wanted now. My father
was Chief Executive; we lived in a five-room apartment
on the twenty-fifth floor in Cuffe Parade.
My problem was how to suffer, for I knew
suffering to be essential to art; and yet

there was little cause for suffering; I had loving parents
and everything I required. I disowned our Mercedes-
Benz, took the 106 bus, but remained
unable to solve my lack of want.
I pretended to be poor; I wore khadi.
My parents hosted ever larger parties.
I grew thin and consumptive worrying about the absence
of poverty in my life, and the continued, benign
attendance of parents who were good and kind:

all the wrong ingredients, I feared, for the birth
of poetry. Starting to study for O
and A levels, I lost touch with college friends.
Taking long walks down Cuffe Parade towards
Regal Cinema, I only ever visited Elphinstone

College at night, passing the beediwalla
and the bus stop where commuters stood waiting;
here, where once I'd "hung out"
with fellow students, were desultory families,
playing cards on the pavement, each, insouciantly,
revealing their hand to the passerby; prostitutes
glowed palely against pillars guarding the college and Lund
& Blockley, where students at day glanced right
a moment before they crossed the road; and addicts
of smack who loitered between these, speaking
a lingua of broken English and Bombay Hindi,
with whom I opened conversations that ended
in a wry plea for money. They didn't want you for company
but to slip in that plea. We came to know

each other by sight. Thus that curved stretch
before Elphinstone, going past Flora Fountain,
towards Dadabhai Naoroji Road, where the pillars
became Zoroastrian lions, containing their power,
the banks closed, the odd mix of activity
and purpose at eleven-thirty at night, the road
seeming to widen on the left where my school
and childhood and the sugarcane-juice stall used to be.
Nineteen eighty-three, I left for England. In '85,
on my annual trip home, searching for the car
in the parking lot in Kala Ghoda between
Rhythm House and the Jehangir Art Gallery, I heard

my name being called out: "Amit." I turned
and saw it was Suresh beckoning to me

from behind the Ambassador. I went up to him
and said, as if I were seeing him after a fortnight's absence
from school, "Suresh! Where have you been?"
"Good to see you—where are you these days?" He was taller
than me now: about six feet tall,
good-looking, if dressed in average working clothes,
crouched behind the car as if he were hiding behind it.
"I'm in England—I'm back for a few months—
but tell me about yourself." As the art crowd in kurtas
ascended the wide steps of the Gallery, he lowered
his voice melodramatically: "I'm fucked,
yaar. I need help. Amit, will you be my friend?"
Disarmed by this straightforward appeal, I asked,
"Why, what's the matter?" as if I'd already said "Yes"

to the question. Truth to tell, I needed a friend
myself at that time. We go to each other
from our own private compulsions. I've seldom
been wholly comfortable or open
with people who share my background or "interests"
and have ended up acquiring an eclectic set
of companions. "I'm on smack, yaar," he said.
There were no outward signs. He had shaved; his trousers
were conventionally pressed; his hair combed back
and oiled. "So it's true, what I heard. How did it
happen?" "It happened in Elphi . . ." We were walking;
he nodded to the stall with cigarettes and Frooti
tetrapacks beyond the BEST terminus,
and the scurrying ragpickers beside it. "Those bastards are
     pushers.

A friend from Elphi said, 'Just have a drag, yaar.' "
He shook his head with a sort of pride. "That's how
I got hooked. That bastard, if I could take my re-
re-revenge . . ." He looked oddly pleased with himself,
compromised only by the blip of the stammer
that would infrequently return, like a signal,
to his speech, and once made one or two girls giggle.
I entered his life; saw him join "rehab" with Dr.
Yusuf Merchant, get his father to pay
for both his habit and his rehabilitation
—his father, whom he so resembles, both of them
complaining about each other and bickering
like a married couple—try to escape to Dubai
or to hotel management or a brief job as a Blue Dart

courier; during clear intervals
reluctantly "help" his father with his small-time
but extant business, making industrial accessories.
What foolish illusion made that man
put his son in Cathedral, among the children of the Tatas,
minor ministers, consuls, film actors
and actresses (Nutan's son; I remember her waiting
for him, thin and nervous, in slacks, after school;
Sunil Dutt's daughter, gentle, with kohl
in her eyes)? Three sisters; the youngest got married
and moved to Prabhadevi; a tame and stable marriage
after infatuation and heartbreak with a German. The oldest,
whose sexual persuasion Suresh claimed he wasn't sure of,
emigrated to Germany; the one in the middle

stayed single, and works for a travel agent, one
of the two rented rooms this family lives in
in Colaba, partitioned between brother and sister.

"Why doesn't she go away?" he'd ask
irately as he shaved. He would cut himself—tiny
nicks like spattered paint, wash himself with soap.
He never applied aftershave. This boxer
was afraid of its sting. I gave him a T-shirt
that said "Oxford University" in white Gothic letters;
he wore it occasionally as he went out into the great,
unruly, smelly stream of life on the Causeway.
He took an inordinately long time getting ready.
Next to him was the oblong bathtub that was used
as storage space for water; brimming idly—

Bombay's perpetual water shortage; the taps
dry for most of the day, the flush
not working. Then going out. Our walks
by turns quarrelsome, silent, jocular,
amidst the crowds that jostled before the Taj, where on other
days I'd sit in the Sea Lounge, listening
to the piano; now pressing past balloon sellers
and pushers, to whom he claimed he was immune
in my company. My father retired, and later
my parents moved from this city; they sold
their lovely post-retirement flat in St. Cyril Road
in Bandra. And Suresh kept "slipping" and going
back to smack. "An addict can smell out drugs anywhere
he is," he boasted. Britannia Biscuits

had changed, as things do, been touched by scandal, in a tussle
for power between two share-buying players,
a textile tycoon, Nusli Wadia, Jinnah's
grandson, and a Singaporean cashew prince, ending
in the latter's arrest and his death in prison.
"Take me out of here," said Suresh, meaning "Colaba."

When we come to Bombay these days—my wife,
myself, and our infant daughter—we stay
in either the Yacht or WIAA Club or
are put up for a few nights at the President Hotel
—this five-star orphanage or dharamshala—
when my book readings beckon. We go to see Suresh
in his room in Colaba, or he comes to see us;
he's still shy with my wife, and would rather speak with me,

but makes dramatic attempts to win over my daughter.
He's going bald. Since I've no home in this city,
we stop for lunch and wonton soup
at the Bombay Gymkhana, whose verandah is the only
place I can put down this mewling, regurgitating
baby on a wicker chair. People
around us are eating; the curious mix
of children from Cathedral School and lawyers
and managers and society ladies and poets
like Imtiaz Dharker, and editors of newspapers.
Not infrequently, I run into
old school friends or acquaintances
like Anurang Jain, one of the twins,
Anurang and Tarang, who now lives in

Aurangabad, a businessman,
or Anant Balani, film producer,
still awaiting his big success,
or Saran, who always says "Hello"
although I didn't know him very well in school.
It's odd how the bullies have calmed down, how
the slimes and duds and good guys have
alike transformed into gentlemen,
or moderate successes, or ordinary

executives. There's Shireen—who was
in my class before I was transferred
to B, both of us teased pitilessly
because she lived on the floor below me in
Il Palazzo. Her father, an irascible

cardiologist, practised the violin furiously
for relaxation. My friends burst into "Knock three
times on the ceiling if you want me"
whenever they saw her to embarrass me.
The first flush of that shame's over. She's
a solicitor, and looks assured. "Amit,"
brown hair around her freckled face, "I read about you
in the papers." She's nicer than I can ever remember.
After this, we ignore each other, no longer
burdened with having to fulfil the jejune
prophecy of that popular song. Suresh
comes regularly if reluctantly
(apprehensive of whom he'll run into),
and shares chicken Manchurian and

fried rice. Each day we study the menu.
This is the last stop on my book tour.
Suresh has been seven years "clean," ever since
his mother, whom he loved more than anyone else
(and whom he also blames for loving him—
"She made me weak"), this short, round-bellied
Mangalorean woman, for whom a picture
of the Madonna is illuminated
in their drawing room, died; she had a congenital
heart murmur not unlike the one I was born with,
which tired her at times and made her look absent;
she was too old to operate on. This—her life's soft

companion—didn't kill her; one day
her synthetic negligee caught fire

as she was heating milk on the stove. Suresh,
who was still flirting with smack, spending more time
at home than at work, overheard her screams
and saw her from the ventilator windows
above the doors to the other room, which
were locked. Since then, he's stopped "taking," and
they commemorate her death once a year, the father,
the son, and the still single sister, whom he
still resents but accepts now, philosophically;
though in what way the sight of a mother burning
should be a reprimand to an old habit,
I don't know. Anyway, he has not the means
to compose her a more fit epitaph than this,
this second attempt to return, like a prodigal

son, to "normal life," for her sake
and his, though "normal life," rediscovered,
is an empty promise filled with cars and people
and noises that frighten him slightly. He tells me
how fourteen years of semi-oblivion and a sort
of absence have left him maladjusted
and inept and unsure of himself. The book tour
goes on even after it's supposed to be over; reporters
who haven't read my book come and ask me questions.
It's Valentine's Day. Elsewhere in the city,
the Shiv Sena is burning Valentine cards.
Here, in the Gymkhana, young couples hold hands
and look wide-eyed and unnaturally devout and composed.
Evening brings the dark to the maidan, and, with it,

mosquitoes. This morning, we mentioned Sujata
Birla, rhetorically. "Hey, d'you remember
Sujata?" "Yeah," in a tone of disbelief,
"she died in a plane crash, yaar." We already
know this, how she married after college, was divorced,
then married again—a happy flowering; on that plane
were her mother and her father, Ashok Birla. The husband
wasn't with them that day. I pick up my daughter
and we head for Pipewalla Building in a taxi,
my wife carrying the feeding beaker and the packet
with the sari she bought from Cottage Industries
earlier today. For her, this city
means shopping expeditions, leather handbags
to admire in Csango, which she'll visit even if

she buys nothing, only inspects and desires.
"Looking at" costs nothing; but the proprietor
doesn't mind, as if he knows it's somehow connected
to business. Then the haunts whose names
she's inherited from my parents; the incredibly Olympian
Joy Shoes; R. H. Rai; Ramniklal Zaveri
to exchange an old ornament; from shop to shop, as
the book tour fizzles out, and we find we're at a loose end
with two days left in this city, and nowhere
to go. Suresh has promised to take us
for dhansak to the Paradise Café. Here, by the entrance
near the Kodak Studio on the main road, is the shrine,
already wet with religious dousings and drownings,
and a small driveway where Suresh's scooter

is parked. He lives on the second floor; on the third
is a guest house where Iranians and Arabs put up.

Below, in the compound, is a detached room
which, for five years, has been a Shiv Sena office. Tonight
it wears a lit and festive air. Two policemen
have been posted by the gates, as if to say
"We're taking no chances." When one of them, corpulent
and whiskered, smiles at my daughter (she, at a year
and a half, is a veteran talker and walker, and
wanders near him), I feel a disquiet.
She smiles back at him, as if it's possible
to make friends with the intractable. He relaxes;
glances at me. Is he guarding the Sena
or against it? We go to the building, conferring,
making sure not to look back over our shoulders.

Chasing a Poet: Epilogue

"He hangs out at the Wayside Inn till four."
Thus, Adil, whose eye, looking away,
promises, says a young poet, to conceal something.
Leave this watering hole behind, Bombay Gym,
and take my wife and half-sleeping child
in a taxi towards Jehangir Art Gallery.
Installations this week in Kala Ghoda.
"You'd better move fast, if you want to catch him," Adil
says, consulting, in his squinty, alien way,
my watch. In the Inn, I don't see him at first,

Kolatkar, his face youthful, his eyes
baleful, like a student's, his hair and moustache
grey-white, as if they were made of cotton wool, a prankster's
disguise. He's concealed in the shadows, open
to strangers, but forewarned of me.
The Inn's semi-deserted; the famous smell
of fish and chips has disappeared; some of the chairs
and tables have been enlisted for a reading
tonight. I go up, to introduce myself
before Thursday ends, and this man melts away.

He's about seventy years old; he
appraises me as a college boy would a teacher
who's interrupted him smoking marijuana.
He says he's heard of me; invites
me to sit down. "I saw your poster
in Crossroads yesterday. You're reading day after,
aren't you?" (All these new bookshops

and shopping malls—Crossroads, Crosswords—
where books and CDs and stationery and toys
are sold in busy neighbourliness. And exhortations
to go to Lotus. "Have you been to Lotus? It's quite
far away, but it's a *real* bookshop. The books
are fantastic!") I've been trying to track down this
man to persuade him to let my publishers
reissue his first book of poems, *Jejuri*,
a sequence, published in '76, about a visit
to the obscure, eponymous pilgrimage town

in Maharashtra. Arvind Mehrotra says it's
"the best-loved book of poems by an Indian writer
in English," or words to similar effect, with good
reason. He confesses his shyness of contracts
while ordering me a coffee. We're joined
by a bespectacled itinerant from the ad world, who
has an omelette and toast. "But if you're involved . . .
I don't mind." I try not to interrupt as he
drifts lazily into conversation with the spectacled man,
but ask him to keep a signed copy of

Freedom Song: Three Novels rather shamefacedly.
He does not demur; he studies its cover.
I tell him I must retrieve wife and daughter
from Rhythm House, and brave the traffic
to Mahim, to take part in a "live chat"
on rediff.com. "I've never done this sort
of thing before." He suggests I protest
too much. "I think Amitabh and Jaya
Bachchan were on it the other day," he says, smiling
smokily; I see myself in a mirror,

dishevelled, late. What is it exactly
that I want from him? Neither he nor I
quite know, and we know that we don't know,
and this lack of certainty, in which he has the mild
upper hand, this bogus talk about
contracts, I suppose, gives us some
leverage with each other, or is that only my
fancifulness? We agree to meet for lunch
on Monday, a day before I fly
back to Calcutta. For twenty-five years

he's published nothing, or little. This doesn't mean
he's not been writing. In fact, for many years,
he's been composing poems about the Kala Ghoda
he sees from his window at the Wayside Inn,
the parking lot now cleared of cars for the ten-day
festival. He writes about the woman
who washes herself and her children, and cooks
on the pavement, or the homeless stringing their string cots,
or odd-job men and their paramours

and quick lunches. As I discover on Monday,
when the Wayside Inn's full, and we crowd
round a single table, lunch is a great
unspoken theme. People enter, leave,
sated or still in search of satiation;
Arvind will send me some poems a couple
of months later, by Kolatkar, describing the slop
eaten by the odd-job man on the pavement.
We are united by orders of dhansak and fish
and chips, and kachumbar, drowned out by cries of "Waiter!"
and "Arrey, Udwadia?" I think of Frank O'Hara,

like Kolatkar, between the painter's world and the poet's
(Kolatkar is a well-known commercial artist),
writing his "lunch poems," crossing the streets
from Times Square to Sixth Avenue in New York
on weekdays, a cheeseburger in one hand,
Poems by Pierre Reverdy in one pocket.
Kala Ghoda, in those poems I've still
to read, is no less beautiful in its journey
between the Jehangir Art Gallery and the Wayside Inn.
"Neon in daylight is a / great pleasure," says O'Hara
as he discovers its useless radiance around mid-day.
Kolatkar notes a different flame. "They're burning
Valentine cards today," gravely
in his deep Bombay accent, musical
with irony. And "Arvind's begun
to look like Gurudev Tagore." Pauses. "By
the way, will your daughter have ice cream?" My wife
gratefully accepts. Our mealtime's not
quite over; while a half a lifetime's work is almost
done, and remains concealed, as if it were
ingested, and coursing in the veins; and another's
half a lifetime's work still to begin;
no hunger, before or after lunch, is complete.

Note

Two stories here are retellings—and quite personal interpretations—of episodes from the Hindu mythologies. "An Infatuation" is a retelling of an episode from the *Ramayana*, in which Lord Ram (often spelt Rama) is exiled to the forest for fourteen years because of a curse; he is accompanied by his brother Lakshman and his wife, Sita. Here, a rakkhoshi (the Bengali word for female rakkhosh, or rakshas in Hindi—a powerful demon), Surpanakha, falls in love with him and tries to seduce him. Ram plays along with her and then humiliates her, as the episode shows. She rushes to her brother Ravan, the king of demons, who will avenge her by abducting Ram's wife, Sita—thus setting into motion the main action of the *Ramayana*. "The Wedding" is a retelling of the story of Lord Shiv's (often spelt Shiva) wedding.

Most of the other stories are set in either Bombay or Calcutta, at any time between the seventies and the present, with the exception of "The Great Game," which is set in both Bombay and the city of Sharjah, in the United Arab Emirates. The Hindi word "saala" in the story literally means "brother-in-law"; but it is also a term of abuse. In a casual sense, it suggests someone who has the tiresomeness of a brother-in-law; in a stronger vein, it carries the implication "I have slept with your sister." I should point out that the story was composed some time before the match-fixing controversy in early 2000, in which key players from several countries were either found to have thrown, or were suspected of throwing, matches in return for payment from bookies. This story is not about match fixing, but it does depict the one-day game (as opposed to the more traditional "test" match, played over five days), in which there is always a result. The rise of the one-day game has been coterminous with the globalisation and commodification of the sport, its incursion into unlikely places, and the spread of satellite television.